# DEADLY HARMONY

A
GEORGIA RAE WINSTON
MYSTERY

## MARISSA SHROCK

### CIMELIAPRESS

Published by Cimelia Press, Greentown, Indiana

Printed in the United States of America

Print ISBN-13: 978-0-9969879-5-0

Library of Congress Control Number: 2019911891

Why, my soul, are you downcast? Why so disturbed within me? Put your hope in God, for I will yet praise him, my Savior and my God.

Psalm 42:11

## AUTHOR'S NOTE

One of the best aspects of being a writer is imagining a story world. Richard County, Webster County, Wildcat Springs, and Richardville are all fictional places, though I did use Indiana history and geography when I created the names. I also utilized some fictional license with police procedures to remain true to the pace of the story.

# CHAPTER ONE

Nineteen days. Two hours. And approximately thirty minutes.

That was all the time it'd taken for Cal to move on? I ducked behind a brick column in Smithson's Steakhouse and calculated my next move while my ex-boyfriend was immersed in conversation with Taryn Anderson—the cute baker from my hometown of Wildcat Springs, Indiana.

I glanced over my shoulder. Taryn giggled and twirled her blond hair, which she'd released from her usual perky top knot. Just my luck. I hadn't seen Cal since our breakup, and the first time I ran into him, he was on a date?

This was precisely why I didn't gamble.

I curled my fingers into a fist and lamented my need for the restroom. Why didn't I have a bladder of steel? Why had I ventured from the safety of the booth I was sharing with my best friend, Brandi Hartfield?

Brandi caught my eye, and confusion played in her expression when she saw my back pressed flat against the column as if I were an awkward spy in a cheesy, made-for-TV movie. I gave a single nod to my left, and understanding dawned in her face.

Then she laughed.

My normally compassionate and motherly friend was getting quite the chuckle at my expense.

I glared at her, and she motioned toward Cal and Taryn's table.

Brandi thought I was going to saunter over and talk to them? "No way," I mouthed.

She took a drink of water.

Easy for her to give advice, but I shouldn't be too hard on her. She'd faced her share of romantic woes. After being single for many years, she'd married, only to be widowed a few years later.

Our waiter, wearing a cowboy hat, emerged from the kitchen with our food. My stomach rumbled as he set the plates on our table. Filet mignon was calling my name.

I sneaked a peek at Cal's table again and back at Brandi who flicked her fingers toward Cal. It would take every ounce of strength for me to walk across the restaurant.

I closed my eyes as the world carried on around me. Clinking silverware punctuated muffled conversations. "Refund" wailed through the speakers. Even though I hated country music, the song was unavoidably popular, and I sang along in my head.

*Give me a love refund. Reimburse this sad affair. My forevermore has just begun. Repay each day I dared to care.*

Maybe I didn't mind the song because I related it to my situation with Cal. I wasn't getting any younger, and sometimes it felt like I'd wasted precious time on him.

I opened my eyes and wiped my sweaty palms against my jeans. All I needed to do was smile and act like the thirty-one-year old, independent woman I was. Ending the relationship had been my idea, and if Taryn had better luck getting Cal to open up about his life, then more power to her. I gritted my teeth and crushed a stray peanut shell under my snake-print pumps.

*Help me, Jesus.*

I flipped my honey-blond hair and squaring my shoulders, I marched out into the open and stared at Cal as I strolled toward my table.

As if he sensed my laser-like gaze, he looked up—and away.

*Oh no you don't.* I veered left. *Life Lesson #3009: Refuse to be ignored.*

"Hey, there!" I plastered on a smile as I approached Cal and Taryn's booth.

"Hi, Georgia!" Taryn surveyed me with a triumphant smirk.

Part of me didn't blame her. Detective Cal Perkins was quite a catch with his dimple, dark hair, and stunning blue eyes. Not to mention he was taller than me, and I couldn't say that about a whole lot of men. A former professional baseball player, excellent cook, and detective with the Richard County Sheriff's Department, he was the total package. Everyone in our small town had thought we'd end up married.

However, our relationship had stalled, and when I'd made the decision to end things, it'd seemed like the right one. But seeing him with Taryn would take some getting used to.

"Are you enjoying your dinner? This is such a fun place," I said.

Cal sawed a piece of wheat bread from the loaf, ripped off a bite, and shoved it in his mouth—all without looking at me.

"It's great. I had the cedar plank salmon, and it was delicious." Taryn pointed to her plate.

Three things. First, how anyone could ingest that disgusting pink meat was beyond me. Second, why would anyone get *fish* at a steakhouse? Third, was Cal seriously not going to acknowledge my presence?

I set my jaw. "How's work, Cal?"

"Fine. Things have slowed down since last month." He finally met my eyes, and he'd perfected the Leave-Us-Alone expression.

I was *not* going to let his demeanor get to me. Not Georgia Rae Winston. Nope. Winstons were tough. Resilient. Feisty.

I'd cry later.

"Have a nice evening." I turned on my heels and sailed back to Brandi, hoping I was giving off a casual vibe.

"I'm proud of you." She cut into her steak.

"Because I willingly embarrassed myself?" I slid into the booth.

"You didn't embarrass yourself, and the last time we saw Cal on a date with someone, it took Ashley giving you a pep talk in the restroom to get you to go say hello.

That'd happened before we'd dated, so I was clearly making progress. "What was up with you laughing at me?"

She ducked her head, and her short brown curls bounced. "I'm sorry. I don't know what got into me. But seeing you pressed against the brick column—" She dissolved into giggles.

"I hope you don't do this to your students." I shook out my napkin that looked like a cowboy bandana and spread it over my lap. "You could warp them for life."

She somehow managed to compose herself. "I'm sorry. If it makes you feel any better, I started praying the minute I realized what was happening."

"In between giggles. That's quite a feat." I picked up my fork and met her concerned gaze. "It *did* help." My temporary burst of courage could only be explained by divine origin.

"Good." She tilted her head. "I probably shouldn't tell you this, but Cal couldn't keep his eyes off of you when you walked over here."

I cut into my filet. "That actually makes me feel a *lot* better."

An hour later, Brandi and I made our way through a crowd and took our seats in Wildcat Springs Community Church's auditorium. The massive, modern building was a far cry from the old-fashioned brick church where we'd worshipped when I was a kid.

My twenty-one-year-old stepsister Makayla's college chorale was on a tour headed for Colorado, and tonight was their first concert. Since the students were staying with families from the church, I'd be hosting Makayla and two of her friends. Technically, we were close enough for her to go home to Richardville, but since my mom and her dad were on a mission trip to Guatemala, and their wood floors were being refinished, Makayla was stuck with me.

Brandi answered a text before dropping her phone into her purse. "Dalton made dinner reservations at Salvador's for tomorrow night."

"How are things going?" She'd been on several dates with the physical therapist.

"He's a nice guy." She brushed some lint from her gray pants and glanced around at the gathering crowd. "Hamlet's over there." She smiled and waved at her second cousin and his mom and dad, Bobbi Sue and Hemingway Miller, who sat to our left.

I lifted my handbag from the floor and double checked to see if my phone volume was off. "That's nice."

"Mmm-hmm."

I didn't dare look to see if Brandi was having another laugh at my expense. Instead, I dumped my phone back into my purse and acknowledged Hamlet, though his parents didn't appear to notice me.

As I set my purse back on the floor, the choir demonstrated perfect timing and filed onto the risers on stage. The girls wore black A-line gowns with sweetheart necklines, while the boys sported tuxedoes. As soon as they were in place, they opened with "Sing to the Lord."

The song brought back memories of my college days when I'd majored in music education and traveled with my college's choir. I'd never used my degree to teach. Instead, I'd started farming corn and soybeans with my grandpa after my daddy died and Grandpa had talked about selling the farm.

Not once had I regretted my decision.

The song ended, and as we applauded, I glanced around— and accidentally met Hamlet's steady gaze.

*Stay focused on the music, Georgia Rae.* The last thing I needed was another relational complication when I was trying to heal.

Almost an hour later, the students moved from the stage and circled the auditorium for their final song. As they sang "Give Me Jesus," goosebumps rose on my arms at the beautiful harmonies. The words of the song helped remind me that even if my life wasn't what I wanted it to be, all I needed was Jesus.

I'd been living that truth every day since my breakup with Cal.

The choir hit the closing notes, and I caught my stepsister's eye and smiled as the audience applauded. In the six years I'd known her, we'd never been close, but because my relationship with her identical twin brothers Preston and Austin had improved, I wanted to make progress with her.

Pastor Mark closed with a prayer, and the director thanked those of us who were housing students and told us to meet them in the chapel. People began exiting the auditorium, but quite a few audience members—including Hamlet and his parents— lingered and gabbed with their friends and the students.

"I want to talk to the director," I said to Brandi, and she followed as I fought the stream of people going the opposite way until I stood in front of the stocky, middle-aged man. Since I was too tall for my own good, I towered over him. "Dr. Jackson, I enjoyed the performance. When I was in college, I sang with—"

"Thank you for coming." His well-enunciated words held a faint trace of a British accent. He adjusted his wire-rimmed glasses and looked past me. "Pardon me." He strode toward a man who reminded me of Patrick Swayze.

"That was abrupt," Brandi said.

"No kidding." I surveyed the room. At least our little interaction with the director had given Hamlet and his parents time to move on. Her Royal Awkwardness didn't need a second embarrassing encounter in one night.

"Brandi?" A guy in a paisley button-down shirt lingered next to us. I guessed he was about forty, and his full, reddish-brown beard was flecked with gray.

"Lukas!" Her face glowed, and she hugged him. "It's great to see you again." She kept her hand on his arm and turned to me. "Georgia, this is Lukas Dawes. We graduated from Brenneman together. Lukas, this is Georgia Winston."

We shook hands and exchanged greetings. Lukas wasn't what I'd call handsome, but his smile transformed his face, obliterating any plainness.

"Who are you here to see?" she asked.

"My little brother Jonas. I'm an artist manager based in Nashville. We're kicking off our Midwest tour tomorrow night in Chicago, so I told Jonas I'd come since it's not too far out of my way."

"Who do you manage?" Brandi gazed up at him.

She batted her eyes, which I'd never actually witnessed.

"Parker Curtis."

Brandi's jaw dropped. "My sister Carly and I adore Parker Curtis. What a cool job!"

"It is. Parker's always been fun to work with, and it's getting crazy now that he has a hit song." Lukas grinned. "How about I

7

get you and Carly some free tickets and backstage passes. He's playing in Fort Wayne Sunday night."

She clasped her hands. "Yes, please! That's so generous!"

If we hadn't been standing in a crowded church, I was ninety-five percent certain she would've kissed him.

Lukas removed his phone from his back pocket, and they exchanged contact information. Then he surveyed the thinning crowd. "Do either of you know the way to the chapel? I'd like to say *hey* to my brother before I head out."

"Sure. We have some guests to pick up." I led the way through the auditorium and back hallway to the chapel.

Brandi and Lukas trailed behind and chatted about life and how they'd lost touch. When we entered the chapel, the students stood in clusters next to stacks of luggage, and several of them waited in the pews.

A slim kid with a sparse beard waved at Lukas as he approached us. "Hey, bro." Jonas hugged Lukas. "Let me finish the housing assignments, and we'll talk." He motioned down at the tablet he was holding.

"No problem. These ladies need to pick up some students." Lukas nodded. "Nice to see you again, Brandi." He hugged her again. "I'll be in touch about the tickets." He took his phone out of his pocket and walked away.

"Take care." Her gaze lingered on Lukas before she snapped her attention to Jonas. "Brandi Hartfield."

Jonas consulted his tablet. "Got it." He motioned to a group of four girls gathered next to a pew. "You'll be hosting Taylor, Kenzie, Jessa, and Dani. Feel free to leave as soon as you're ready. Please have the girls back here tomorrow morning at eight sharp."

"Will do." Brandi turned to me. "Have a good one." She walked over to the girls and greeted them.

We'd definitely discuss Lukas as soon as possible because I needed details. I checked in with Jonas and then scanned the crowded room. I zeroed in on my stepsister, and she shot a tight smile in my direction. Her blue-green eyes were her most striking feature, and she'd toned down the pink streaks in her brown, shoulder-length hair and lost the lip ring she'd added before Thanksgiving. The petite black girl standing next to her gave me a friendly smile. They waited next to a pile of suitcases, coats, and bookbags.

"Sammi, this is my stepsister, Georgia." Makayla hitched her thumb in my direction. "Georgia, Sammi Cardwell."

Sammi held out her hand. "Nice to meet you. We appreciate you taking us in for the night." Her brown eyes sparkled.

"You're welcome." I scanned the crowd. "Where's your other friend?"

Makayla and Sammi glanced around.

"Her bags are here." Sammi furrowed her brow and then turned. "Oh, there she is." She waved at a slender girl with a pixie haircut, nose ring, and a sulky expression. "Quincy! Over here!"

Quincy shoved her hands into her skirt pockets and threaded her way through the groups of people. "I was in the restroom," she mumbled. Grabbing her backpack from the luggage pile, she swept her gaze over me. "I take it you're Georgia."

"Yes. Nice to meet you, Quincy." I turned to the other girls. "Is everyone ready?"

"Absolutely!" Sammi grabbed her suitcase handle.

Makayla picked up her red, 1980s vinyl raincoat and threw it over her arm. "Fine with me."

"Yep." Quincy glanced at her phone and slung her backpack over her shoulder.

The last bit of orange daylight edged the western horizon as I led them outside to my truck. For late March, the evening was unseasonably warm, and earlier that day, the temperatures had soared into the low seventies. I knew better than to get used to the balminess, because a cold front was projected to sweep in, and snow flurries were forecasted for tomorrow night.

Since they were wearing formal dresses, I hefted their suit-cases into my truck bed while they piled into the extended cab. Sammi took shotgun when Makayla refused.

I followed the winding drive out of the parking lot and turned onto the rural highway. Only an occasional house, barn, or grove of trees broke up the flat, fertile land crisscrossed by grids of roads.

Awkward silence paid us a visit, and all three girls kept their faces buried in their phones. *Good grief.* Though I didn't live too far from the church, it'd sure seem like a long trip if someone didn't talk.

Fortunately, babbling was my specialty.

"You all did such a nice job tonight. I loved singing in my college choir, and we took some of the best tours. We went to New York, and I even got to go to England one spring break. Oh, the stories I could tell. One time we were singing in this cathe-dral, and as we were walking in, my foot hit the prayer railing, and it echoed so badly through that old building. That made me want to laugh, which is the worst feeling in the world when you can't because everyone is so serious and quiet." I took a breath.

"I definitely know the feeling." Sammi giggled.

At least one of them had listened to my yammering. "Are you excited about the tour?" I glanced in the rearview mirror.

"No." Quincy didn't bother to look up from her phone. "I'd rather be going to the beach in Florida. I've already been to Colorado like a hundred times."

*Must be rough.* "Do you, *like*, have family there?" *Bad Geor-gia. Bad, bad Georgia.*

"No, but I know a great resort in Miami Beach." Her thumbs flew over the phone.

"Sammi? Makayla? What about you?"

In the back seat, Makayla shrugged. "A beach would've been my choice too, but whatev."

"I've never been to Colorado." Sammi rested her phone in her lap. "I'm excited to see the mountains. They've even scheduled a day for us to snow ski, and I've never done that either, even though I'm from Michigan. My family's into water skiing." She smiled as if she were trying to compensate for her friends' surly attitudes.

*Okay, then.* Frankly, I was puzzled. Brenneman University was a Christian college, and Quincy—and even Makayla—had a little more edge than I'd been expecting. Maybe I was being naïve. After all, Quincy could've been on the let's-fix-our-kid-by-sending-her-to-a-Christian-school plan.

Because that was so effective.

"Fun fact about my stepsister," Makayla said. "She's a detective."

Now she was talking me up? Where in the world did that come from?

"Wait, what?" Quincy looked up from her phone. "I thought she's, like, a farmer."

"Well, that's how she makes money, but she's solved several murder cases in her spare time."

"Cool." Sammi's eyes lit up. "Are you a consultant like Shawn Spencer on *Psych*?"

A woman after my own heart. "I love that show, but no." I kneaded the steering wheel. "Mostly, I've been in the right places at the right times. Plus, I enjoy talking to people, and sometimes they give me information—without realizing it." I turned off the highway onto a much narrower—but paved—county road.

"It all started when somebody killed her dad and his case went cold," Makayla said.

Really? Why'd she bring that up? Didn't she realize that was a painful topic? She should've. She'd been ten when her mom had died.

Quincy leaned forward. "Did you find your dad's killer?"

"I had help, but yes. Last month the person was finally caught after nine years." I winced at the memory.

Sammi shook her head. "I'm sorry. That had to have been hard—losing him and not knowing what happened all that time."

"Thank you." It'd been excruciating.

I furrowed my brow as we approached my neighbor's white, two-story house. Why were there lights on? Beverly had passed away last month. Her daughter must be cleaning it out to sell.

My throat thickened at the memory of my dear friend who'd always had a kind word and wise advice. Then I smothered a smile. Cal had adopted Beverly's black schnauzer Miss Peacock. How were they getting along? Did Taryn like yippy dogs? If not, she'd better get used to it.

As I turned into my driveway, gravel crunched under the tires. I'd purchased the one-hundred-year-old farmhouse and surrounding five-acre property from my mom when she'd remarried. Right now, it was a bigger home than I needed, but I hoped someday there'd be kids to bring life into the place.

"I've never stayed on a farm before, but I went on a field trip to one in preschool." Sammi peered out the window in the direction of my old red barn, pole barn, and grain bins. "This is awesome."

"Thanks. Where do you live in Michigan?" I asked.

"Novi—Detroit area."

I opened the garage door and parked next to the old, silver Grand Prix I'd owned for years. I drove the old girl I'd nicknamed Gretel once in a while when I didn't want to feel big and bad in my truck. "I have a very friendly yellow lab named Gus. He's harmless and loves company, so I won't let him out of his crate until you change out of your dresses."

"I love dogs. My family has a golden retriever," Sammi said.

We tromped inside to my 1980s-style kitchen that begged daily for a renovation to be free from flower-basket-print wallpaper and linoleum. Gus howled from his crate in the utility room. "I'll let you out in a minute, buddy."

I led the girls upstairs where I assigned rooms and pointed out the bathrooms and where they could find towels. "If you're hungry, I'll make popcorn, and you can pick a movie." It wasn't that late—at least not what college students would consider late.

"That's perfect. Thank you. I'll be down after I change." Sammi hurried into my brother Dakota's old room.

"I'm gonna crash. What's your Wi-Fi password?" Quincy tapped her phone. "Wait—you have that, right?"

"No. Here in the sticks, we don't depend much on that newfangled technology." My mouth twitched. *Somebody find Nice Georgia, because she's gone on the lam.*

"Oh." Her gazed darted to Makayla.

Makayla rolled her eyes. "She's messing with you."

Quincy let loose a sarcastic chuckle that clearly communicated she was not amused.

She'd obviously forgotten to pack her sense of humor. "There's a card with the password on the nightstand."

She escaped into the guestroom and shut the door.

"You're welcome." I turned to my stepsister. "Well? What about you?"

"I'll be down in a sec." She trudged toward my childhood room.

"Mak?"

"Yeah?" She faced me.

"Are you okay?"

"Yep." She sagged against the door frame.

"Look, I'm sorry you have to stay here instead of—"

"That's not it. Thanks for hosting us."

"No problem." I tried to read her expression but couldn't. Even though her brothers could be supremely annoying, I never had to wonder what they were thinking.

"I need to get out of this dress." She tugged on her skirt and then closed the door.

I headed downstairs to make microwave popcorn—my specialty.

———

A lone soprano sang an *a capella* version of "Give Me Jesus" while a spotlight illuminated her golden hair. Where was I? My surroundings came into focus as the song ended and the house lights came up.

A man wearing a tuxedo stood at the front of my church, but his face was obscured by a paper bag that had *Georgia Rae* written in red block letters. "Why does he have a paper bag on his head?" I muttered.

My stepdad appeared at my side and took my arm.

"Dan? What're you doing here?"

"It's your big day, Georgia." Confusion spread over his handsome face.

*My big* . . . I glanced down and gasped. Where had I gotten this wedding dress? And why was the skirt made of tulle? The fabric invaded half the aisle. Why had my friends let me buy this monstrosity?

Princess material I was *not*.

"It's time." Dan patted my arm.

Brandi, in a fuchsia, puffy-sleeved gown straight from the 1980s, materialized and handed me a bouquet of limp white roses, the petals browned and curled. A crowd filled the auditorium, and I inspected the room, hoping to find a familiar face.

"Who's the groom?" I tried to move my feet, but they remained anchored to the floor.

Dan dragged me forward. "Don't be silly. He's right there." He pointed toward the altar where Pastor Mark waited next to the mystery man.

"*Who's* right there?" My heart thudded, and I couldn't get my feet to work. I stumbled along, clutching Dan's arm.

When we were halfway to the altar, a man in a cowboy hat and bandana burst out of the empty baptistry. He waived an antique silver pistol in the air. "I object!"

Screams rang out when he leveled the gun at Dan and me.

*Bang! Bang!*

I fell as a bloodstain bloomed over my gown's beaded bodice.

A shrill alarm pulsed.

---

I shot up in my bed. With my heart thudding, I clutched my sheets and fanned my pajamas away from my sweaty body. It was just a nightmare.

But the blaring alarm wasn't.

I leaped out of bed.

Gus barked and howled as I sprinted across the living room to the back door and punched in the code for my security system. The shrieking stopped, and I comforted Gus, who rattled and whined in his metal crate.

When Gus calmed down, I entered the kitchen as Quincy, Makayla, and Sammi raced in. All three of them wore short pajama sets.

"I'm *so* sorry." Quincy smoothed her short hair. "This is totally my fault. I got hot and opened a window."

"No, no." I shook my head. "I didn't think about it being too warm." I wasn't exactly a tightwad, but turning on the air conditioning in March seemed downright ridiculous. "I should've told you I set the alarm every night. I'm sorry."

"Some bad guys came after her, so our parents made her get a system," Makayla said.

Sammi froze. "Are we safe here?"

"I'm not in the middle of a case," I said. "So no one should be after me." I cringed. That didn't sound as comforting as I'd hoped.

"We'll be fine," Makayla murmured.

My phone rang.

"Wait, you still have a landline?" Makayla's eyes widened as she whipped her head toward the cordless phone on the kitchen counter.

*Yep. Stick me in a museum next to the dinosaur skeletons.*

"She's not into newfangled technology, remember?" Quincy didn't wrench her gaze from her phone.

"Welcome to the sticks." I answered and reassured my security system company that they didn't need to send someone from the sheriff's department to check on the house.

When I hung up, I glanced at the microwave clock. 12:08. After Sammi, Makayla, and I had eaten popcorn and watched *Psych: The Musical*—Sammi's choice—we'd gone to bed a little before eleven.

"Let's try to get some sleep." Though, with the adrenaline rush I'd experienced, I'd have to swallow a couple of Tylenol PM to even come close to snoozing.

My guests trudged back upstairs, and I took two pills before heading to my room. As I climbed in bed, the memory of my nightmare came roaring back, but I didn't want to think about what that awful dream meant.

"Georgia! Wake up!"

Persistent tapping needled my shoulder. I rolled over and opened my eyes. A wet-haired Makayla hovered over my bed, and I looked at my clock. 6:17. Plenty of time to get the girls breakfast and take them to the church.

"I set my alarm for 6:45," I mumbled as I rubbed my eyes. "If you're hungry, I bought muffins yesterday, and the coffee maker is set to—"

"That's not it." Makayla shook her head, flipping water droplets in my face.

I brushed away the water and blinked. With her arms wrapped around her waist and the same frantic expression on her face, Sammi hovered at my bedroom door. I sat up. "What's wrong, then?"

Distress clouded Makayla's pretty face. "Quincy's gone."

# CHAPTER TWO

"What do you mean Quincy's gone?" I studied my stepsister and Sammi. "This is a prank, right? You got me good. Now let's—"

"This isn't a joke." Sammi launched herself toward the foot of my bed.

"Georgia, I'm like a hundred times more mature than my idiot brothers. There's no way I'd mess with you like that." Makayla's eyes flashed as she crossed her arms.

I blinked. "Right. Sorry. Reflex, I guess." I drew a deep breath, and my eyes fell on my pile of clothes in the corner. I hadn't exactly been expecting guests in my bedroom. Oh well. I had a much bigger issue than my lack of housekeeping skills. "Are you sure she didn't just go out for a run?" Why hadn't I reset the security system?

Because it was unseasonably warm, I'd wanted to let her leave the window open, and I'd thought I could trust three college students.

"Quincy doesn't run," Makayla said.

"A walk in the fresh air? A self-guided tour of my farm?"

Though there wasn't much to see since I didn't keep animals—except for cats who controlled the barn's rodent population and ducks that resided in my pond.

"We've tried texting—and calling." Sammi plucked a thread from her purple, cat-print pajamas. "But she's not answering."

Makayla shook her head. "She took your Grand Prix."

"What?" I croaked. When was the last time I'd driven that old car? Did it even have enough gas? "I can't believe she stole Gretel," I mumbled. Though I did leave the keys hanging on a hook next to the back door. At least she hadn't run off with my truck that was less than a year old.

"I don't know why she didn't use a ride share," Makayla said.

Because she'd been up to no good and didn't want a witness—or a trail. Not to mention, there couldn't possibly have been many drivers available to make the trip to my farm in the middle of the night.

"We asked ourselves the same questions you're going through now." Sammi plopped on the edge of my bed.

I had to find Quincy because there was no way I was going back to church without three girls. The last thing I wanted was to tell Dr. Jackson we'd lost one of his students, even if she *was* an adult. "Walk me through everything that's happened since you woke up."

"I'm a morning person, so I volunteered to make sure everybody was awake on time," Sammi said.

"Quincy sometimes sleeps through her alarm." Makayla sat on the bed next to Sammi. "Once in a while I do too."

"Are you and Quincy roommates?" I needed to pay more attention to Makayla's life.

"Yep."

I turned to Sammi. "Quincy was gone when you went to wake her up."

"Right. I thought she was in one of the bathrooms, but they

were empty. I figured she'd gone to the kitchen to get a drink, so I went to wake up Makayla. She got in the shower, and I went downstairs to make sure Quincy was okay, but she wasn't around."

"By the time I got out of the shower, Sammi was worried, so after she filled me in, I checked your garage."

Interesting how Makayla had immediately thought it was possible Quincy had left. "Makayla, does Quincy have a history of sneaking out?"

"No." She nibbled a hangnail.

I leaned back against my headboard. "Then why check the garage?"

"It was the logical next step," she mumbled.

*Uh-huh.* "Does Quincy have a history of borrowing without asking?"

"Yes. Last week she took that vintage cardigan you got me for Christmas." She huffed. "It's one of my favorites, but she stretched it out because her shoulders are broader than mine."

*Llama-print sweater for the win.* I shoved the thought aside. "Have you texted your friends to see if they know anything?"

"Yeah." Makayla glanced at her phone. "Her boyfriend Jonas hasn't answered."

"Quincy isn't tight with a lot of people in chorale—except Jonas." Sammi checked her phone. "She hangs out with Ava once in a while, so I'll try her." Her fingers flew across the device.

I chewed my lip as I considered my options. The last thing I wanted to do was to report a missing person and stolen vehicle only to have Quincy come bebopping back with an excuse for why she'd needed to borrow my car. "Is her luggage still in the room?"

"Yes." Sammi turned her phone so we could see the screen. "And Ava hasn't heard from her either."

I sighed. "Tell you what. Finish getting ready, because I have to get you to the church. Maybe Quincy needed to run an errand, and she'll be back before it's time to leave."

Makayla and Sammi exchanged glances.

"Okay." Sammi's voice wobbled as she trudged out of my room.

Makayla started to follow but turned back. "I'm sorry."

"Why?" I drilled her with a stare. "None of this is your fault, unless there's something you're not telling me."

"I guess not." She plodded out.

I hopped out of bed, grabbed my cellphone from my nightstand, and tapped Brandi's number. "I lost a kid," I said as soon as she answered.

"What?"

"One of the girls snuck out, stole my car, and no one's heard from her."

"Oh my word. What're you going to do?"

"I don't know. I thought you might have an idea."

"Because I'm a teacher?"

"Yes."

"I've never lost a student, but if I did, I'd contact the parents —and the principal—right away."

"I don't know her parents." I paced in front of my bed. "I'm still in the hoping-she'll-return phase. Will you please ask your guests if they know anything?"

"Are you sure you want word getting out before you talk to the director?"

"It's already out. Makayla and Sammi have been texting their friends."

"Right. Give me a minute. They're eating breakfast."

*Breakfast.*

I put on my robe and slippers and hightailed it to the kitchen where I set chocolate chip grocery store muffins, milk, and juice on the island. No doubt Brandi had made omelets or a fancy casserole, but my guests wouldn't want me to cook. Continental breakfast was safer for all concerned. They weren't even getting muffins from Pastry Delight, because even before Taryn's date with Cal, she'd made me mad enough I'd boycotted her shop.

While I waited for Brandi to finish investigating, I let Gus outside, and he took care of business quickly and scrambled back inside. He wasn't a fan of the dark.

"Georgia?"

"Yeah?"

"The girls haven't heard, but none of them acted surprised Quincy disappeared."

"Why?" I cracked open the plastic muffin container.

"The girls just looked at each other when I asked. Taylor mentioned Quincy had never even talked to her. They all checked social media but came up empty. Dani said she'd heard Quincy likes to bend the rules."

"Thanks for asking."

"No problem. Keep me posted."

We disconnected, and I went upstairs to search for clues in the guest room. Quincy's suitcase yawned open on the floor with a pair of jeans and a sweater crumpled on top. She'd tossed her chorale dress on the chair in the corner. My navy comforter was puddled on the floor next to the bed, and the matching curtain fluttered as chilly air streamed in. I shut the window and rubbed my arms. The heat wave was long gone.

Bending next to the suitcase, I poked around. Plenty of clothes, underwear, and shoes. A cosmetic bag. I tried to remember what Quincy had brought with her the night before.

She'd carried a backpack, but she must've taken it.

*Buzzzz. Buzzzz.*

The suitcase vibrated. Quincy had left her phone? Sure

enough, I found it stashed in the front pocket, which seemed strange. Why not keep it out for easy access?

I sat back on the floor with a sigh. Quincy had been glued to her device the night before, so it was weird she'd leave without it. I pressed the home button and pumped my fist when I didn't need a passcode.

There were messages and missed calls from Ava, as well as Sammi and Makayla. Though guilt pricked my conscience, I checked Quincy's other messages. I figured that a girl who borrowed my car without asking surrendered her right to privacy.

Everything was typical—plans to see movies, questions about class assignments, texts from her mom and grandma checking on her—except there were no messages or recent calls to or from Jonas . . . or any other contact who appeared to be a boyfriend.

Weird. Apparently, they used something else to communicate.

Makayla opened the door to the Jack-and-Jill bathroom that separated the guest room from my old bedroom. "Is that Quincy's?" She knelt next to me.

"Yep. I've been nosing around."

"I can't believe she left without it."

"I know." I tipped it so she could see. "It's also strange that there aren't any texts or calls to Jonas, even though his name is listed in her contacts."

"They used Snapchat a lot."

I handed her the phone. "Be my sidekick and look into that for me. I know nothing about Snapchat." After her brothers had helped me with a case a couple of months earlier, she'd whined about wanting a turn to assist me.

Funny how things were working out.

Her expression grew serious as she investigated. "This is super weird."

"What?"

"I didn't figure I'd find anything helpful since snaps disappear, but I *was* expecting Quincy to have a streak with Jonas."

I must've looked dumbfounded, because she grinned.

"A streak is when you snap someone within twenty-four hours for more than three days in a row. It's a big deal to break a streak. They had a good one going—for a while anyway."

Not knowing this information made me feel very old. "Even if she and Jonas used Snapchat regularly, isn't it weird she doesn't have any texts or calls from him?"

"Super weird."

"Maybe they broke up, and she deleted his old messages?"

Makayla wrinkled her brow. "They were sitting together on the bus yesterday, and she never mentioned a breakup to me." She set the phone on the dresser, and her own phone buzzed. She glanced at it, her shoulders slumping. "Jonas hasn't heard from her either. I guess I should ask him if they're still—"

My doorbell chimed. Gus woofed and scampered for the front door. Makayla and I looked at each other.

"That better be Quincy," I said.

With Makayla at my heels, I tightened my robe and hurried downstairs where Gus circled in the foyer. Since it was still dark, I flipped on the porchlights.

Peering out the sidelight, I gasped. Cal?

"Ohmygoodness. What's *he* doing here?" Makayla whispered. "Do you think he knows about Quincy?"

That wouldn't be good. "I sure hope not." My stomach tightened. What if someone had found Quincy's body? I swiped at the mascara remnants that I was sure were under my eyes, threw the door open, and braced myself for bad news.

"Good morning." My heart blipped—just a teeny bit—at the sight of him.

"Morning." Cal didn't smile.

Did I detect a hint of relief in his expression? He wore

running shorts and a fitted, reflective shirt that showed the muscles in his chest. Clearly, he wasn't on the clock.

And merciful heavens, he looked good.

Refusing to linger on the thought, I gripped the door frame and met his blue eyes. "What's going on?"

"I found your Grand Prix abandoned at Fillmore Cemetery."

# CHAPTER THREE

Sammi rushed downstairs to the foyer. Cal peeked inside my house as the girls huddled together.

"Come in." With a clenching stomach, I stepped aside so he could enter.

He patted Gus on the head and surveyed the three of us. "What's going on?"

"Cal, you remember Makayla." I closed the door.

"Nice to see you." His dimple made a cameo before vanishing.

She flashed a half smile as she patted Sammi's back.

"This is Sammi Cardwell. They're traveling with the Brenneman University Chorale and stayed with me last night—along with their friend Quincy Ashbrook who stole my car sometime after midnight."

"We just figured it out this morning." Sammi sniffed, raised her head, and gaped at Cal—probably the same way I'd looked at His Handsomeness when we'd first met. "Nice to meet you."

"Likewise." He eyed me as if he were trying to decide what to say next.

I figured he was wondering how I always managed to get myself in such messes, and it would be a legitimate question. This was what I got for trying to be hospitable.

"For the last half hour or so, I've been hoping Quincy borrowed my car and would be back before I have to take them to the church at eight. Now that you found the car, and we know she's really missing . . ." I squeezed the bridge of my nose. "Please help us."

I didn't even care that I sounded pathetic.

"Of course. No problem." He rested his hand on my arm.

I hated that his touch was reassuring—and made my heart flutter. *Focus.* "Was there any blood or a sign of a struggle in the car?"

"Not that I could see," he said. "Your car was locked and parked between the road and the fence, but something didn't feel right, so I stopped to look and didn't see anyone."

I shivered at the thought of the creepy old cemetery.

"That's when I ran over here to check on you." His sexy, resonant voice held a note of concern.

"Thanks." I hated the surge of hope that insisted on worming its way into my broken heart. He was an off-duty officer of the law doing his best to protect the community. I studied my fluffy gray slippers. "What should we do?" My brain swam as I tried to piece together an action plan.

"I have a few questions for Sammi and Makayla," Cal said.

"I'll tell you what I can." Sammi tugged the hem of her yellow peasant blouse. "But I don't know Quincy as well as Makayla, so she'll be more help."

"That's fine." Cal turned to Makayla. "How old is Quincy?"

"Twenty." She dropped onto the bench, and Sammi joined her.

"Has she seemed depressed or upset about anything lately?"

"No."

"Has she ever talked about hurting herself?"

"No."

"Does she have a problem with drugs or alcohol?"

"Not that I'm aware of."

Interesting how Makayla had left the door open on that answer.

"Does she ever use drugs?"

Makayla studied her brown ankle booties. "Possibly. But never in front of me."

"Has she ever mentioned running away?" he asked.

"No."

"She did say she'd rather be at the beach in Florida than on our tour." Sammi looked as if it pained her to say anything negative about Quincy.

Makayla nodded. "She mentioned the same thing to me more than once, but I figured she was just complaining. I didn't take her seriously."

"I see." Cal glanced at me. "I'd like to get a look inside your car." I could tell he wanted to say more but was holding back.

"Good idea." I tucked a strand of hair behind my ear. "We can stop there on the way to the church."

"Actually, it would be best if you gave me your spare keys, and I—"

"I'll hurry and get dressed, and we'll all go. Makayla and Sammi, pack up Quincy's things, and give Cal her phone. He might find something we missed."

Cal sighed. "Yes. Bring me her phone."

"On it." Makayla said as they darted upstairs.

I hurried to my bedroom, praying an inspection of my car would tell us something helpful, because I wasn't looking forward to breaking this news to Dr. Jackson.

The cemetery was located roughly two miles north of my house at the edge of a large wooded area. Floyd Fillmore had made his fortune during the natural gas boom of the 1880s and had longed to be buried on a piece of land his granddaddy had owned. With his newfound wealth, he'd purchased the land and created the burial ground. Beginning with Floyd, members of the wealthy Fillmore clan had buried their dead here for most of the late eighteen and early nineteen hundreds.

The Wildcat Springs History Museum had recently paid to refurbish the headstones, but the place had always creeped me out because of the massive weeping willow lurking over the graves and the pretentious wrought iron fence. Not to mention, Floyd's massive, angel-shaped monument in the center towered above the other markers as if it were keeping guard.

Hints of pink-streaked daylight brightened the horizon as I parked my truck on the edge of the gravel path leading to the gate, and Cal, Makayla, Sammi, and I got out. Cal donned disposable gloves that I supplied from the first aid kit in my truck—just in case this turned out to be more than a bored college student running away. Then, he took my spare keys and flashlight and unlocked my old silver coupe.

While he inspected the car, we watched as the wind whipped around us. The willow tree's branches swung in time with the gusts. The raw morning made me wish for yesterday's beautiful weather.

Cal bent next to the driver's seat. When he stood, he held up a brown paper napkin so we could see. "Take a look."

We huddled around him and read the note scrawled on the napkin.

Georgia,

I'm sorry I borrowed your car, but I figured it'd be okay locked up in the sticks. Mak and Sammi, something came up

29

that I have to take care of, so I've got to go. Don't worry about me. I'm totally fine and will be back when school starts. Tell Dr. J. I'm sorry about the tour.

Q

"Is this Quincy's handwriting?" I snapped a picture of it.

Makayla studied the note. "Definitely."

Cal put the note back in the car before popping the trunk and inspecting it.

Sammi's eyes were wide. "What if someone made her write it?"

"It's possible." My gut screamed *no*. "But her tone is casual. Almost flippant. Does she always sign her notes *Q*?"

"Yeah. That's typical, so she's not communicating a hidden message." Makayla shoved her hands in her vinyl raincoat. "In fact, the whole note sounds like normal Quincy. Everything is always all about her." She snapped her mouth shut and pulled up her hood.

"I can't believe she'd do this to us—and to Dr. J." Sammi fiddled with her trench coat belt.

"I don't want to be around when he finds out," Makayla murmured.

"Now this is interesting." Cal held up a pink leather wallet with a single key dangling from it.

"That's Quincy's," Makayla said.

Cal examined the contents. "Her student ID. Two credit cards. And her driver's license. No cash." He slipped the cards out and glanced at them. "Did she have cash with her?"

"Yes. A whole wad." Makayla rolled her eyes. "Before we left Brenneman, we made a gas-station run to get gummy bears. When she was paying, she dropped a hundred-dollar bill. I told her she needed to be careful carrying that much money."

"Does she have a fake ID?" he asked.

"I don't know."

*Interesting question.*

He shoved the cards into the wallet and looked back and forth between Sammi and Makayla. "Ladies, if there's anything you're not telling me, now's the time to share."

Sammi shook her head.

Makayla shuffled her feet against the gravel and heaved a sigh. "Last year when we were in London during our spring break tour, Quincy snuck out of our bed and breakfast to meet her boyfriend Jonas at a pub." Makayla brushed her hair out of her face. "Even though they were the legal age in the UK, Brenneman makes us sign a conduct pledge that says we won't drink."

I crossed my arms. I wasn't thrilled that my stepsister had lied, but I'd deal with that later.

Makayla shifted. "She would've been happier at a school without so many rules, but both of her parents are Brenneman grads—and big donors. I don't think they gave her a choice when it came to college. I've kept being her roommate because I want to be a good example, and she can be a lot of fun, but . . ."

"This isn't how most Brenneman students act," Sammi added quickly. "None of us are perfect, but most of us want to serve and honor God." She shot a nervous smile in Cal's direction.

"I know," he said. "My cousin Kelsey went there and is working as a missionary nurse in Ethiopia."

I chewed my lip, surveyed the graveyard, and considered everything that'd happened. "It's almost like Quincy came here to meet somebody but intended to return. Otherwise, she could've left her wallet at my house with her phone and suitcase if she was planning to run away." I walked around my car. "She learned something that changed her mind and made her leave with the mystery person. She found what she could to write the note, and the napkin fluttered off the seat when she closed the door." I stopped and looked at Cal. "What do you think?"

"That's plausible. Right now, I'm not seeing any evidence that she was taken against her will. Sometimes adults leave and don't want anyone to find them."

---

When Dr. Jackson studied the picture of Quincy's note on my phone, his pudgy face turned a purplish red, and he reminded me of a cartoon character with steam spewing from his ears.

"How did you allow this to happen?" His crisp voice sliced through the high-ceilinged chapel as he directed a scowl at me.

The chattering in the room died off, and the students and hosts in the room turned to stare. As if they'd anticipated Dr. Jackson's reaction, Makayla and Sammi had taken refuge in the restroom.

Cal edged closer to my side.

"How?" My face heated as I gripped the back of a pew. "I opened my home to one of your students who, of her own free will, chose to sneak out and borrow my car without permission." I wasn't going to let this man intimidate me—I'd dealt with arrogant professors like him before. I flipped my braid over my shoulder and stared at him. "This wasn't the type of behavior I was expecting when I agreed to host college students."

He flinched and tugged his collar. "Yes. My apologies. This sort of nonsense isn't what I expect from my students, and I can assure you we've never had an incident like this before," he sputtered. "If the note you found is genuine, then Miss Ashbrook has committed a serious act that will involve discipline from school administration. If she wrote the note under duress, then my primary concern is her well-being."

"Ours too." I motioned to Cal. "This is Detective Calvin Perkins from the Richard County Sheriff's Department. When he was out running, he found my car abandoned at Fillmore Cemetery."

Cal shook Dr. Jackson's hand. "You're free to file a missing person report at any time—if you feel she's in danger."

Dr. Jackson glanced at my phone and then back up at Cal. "Have you found evidence that this disappearing act wasn't Miss Ashbrook's idea?"

"No, sir," Cal said.

"We've made commitments to churches to come and perform, and a great deal of time and energy has gone into planning this tour." Dr. Jackson looked at the ceiling. "Yet I want to make sure Miss Ashbrook is safe." He handed me my phone.

"I understand, sir." Cal said. "I'm sure you'll want to contact her parents and let them know what's happened. They can decide if they want to file a report."

"Yes. That makes sense. They're very hands on and will want to be involved." The purple hue in his face receded. "I'll consult university administration to decide whether or not to continue with our tour."

"That's wise." Cal removed his phone from his pocket. "If you don't mind, I'd like to ask a few questions about Quincy before you make your calls."

"Certainly," Dr. Jackson said.

I started to walk away.

"Hold on, Miss Winston." Dr. Jackson extended a business card. "Call me immediately if you should hear from Miss Ashbrook."

"I will." I tucked his card in my purse, wandered a few feet away, and parked next to the sound board—where I could listen without being obvious. Many of the students displayed worried expressions as they gathered in groups, whispering and glancing around. Others were simply preoccupied with their phones.

Since not a single chorale member wore jeans, I assumed Dr. Jackson must've implemented a strict dress code.

"Did Quincy show any strange or unusual behaviors lately?" Cal asked.

"Not that I'm aware of, though you'll want to speak with her boyfriend Jonas when he arrives." Dr. Jackson smoothed the lapel on his jacket. "Miss Ashbrook is flighty, but I never imagined she'd do something like this."

"What do you know about her background?"

"She's from Indianapolis. The elder Miss Ashbrook attended Brenneman and sang with my chorale. She's very steady and dependable—nothing like her younger sister." He bristled.

"Anything else?" Cal asked.

"Miss Ashbrook is a junior music major. She sings alto. She took my composition class last semester and my music theory class as a freshman." He adjusted his musical-note tie. "I don't mean to appear insensitive, but I have fifty-nine other students in my group, and while I take a professional interest in my students, I don't delve into their personal lives. It simply isn't prudent in this day and age."

"I understand." Cal typed some notes in his phone.

I assumed Dr. Jackson was referring to inappropriate relationships between students and faculty or fear of false accusations from female students, but he didn't appear to be the type young women would flock after. Maybe a British accent covered a multitude of sins.

I wasn't so sure.

"I'd like to talk to her boyfriend Jonas," Cal said.

"Mr. Dawes is arriving now." Dr. Jackson pointed at the young man with the sparse beard who'd helped Brandi and me the night before. "Do you have any other questions?"

"Not at this time."

"Then please excuse me while I phone Quincy's parents."

He adjusted his messenger bag strap and slipped down the hallway.

I trailed Cal as he walked toward Jonas, but Makayla and Sammi blocked my path.

"I need to tell you something." Makayla tugged her sweater sleeves over her hands.

I was only ten years older than her, but I was starting to feel like a surrogate parent and wondered how to address the fact that she'd lied earlier. "Go ahead." I mentally braced myself.

"I'll give you a minute." Sammi joined a group of girls sitting in the pews.

Makayla leaned against the wall. "Last night when I was upset, it was because Quincy and I haven't been getting along, and I wasn't thrilled that we're tour roommates. I'd been hoping to have a break from her."

"I'm sorry. Why aren't you getting along?"

"She's been staying out until like three in the morning. We don't have a curfew, so it's not against the rules. It's just super annoying because she wakes me up when she comes in."

"Is she sneaking around with Jonas?"

"I don't know. Every time I asked where she'd been, she wouldn't tell me." She looked around and lowered her voice. "But Jonas is here now, so I'm not sure he's involved in what went down last night—and I haven't had a chance to ask why he hasn't been communicating with Quincy."

Was Quincy entangled in something bigger—and more sinister—than an illicit meet up with her boyfriend? "Anything else?"

"I'm sorry I lied this morning. I don't know why I covered for Quincy. Especially when she's always doing her own thing." She tucked her hair behind her ears. "I guess I'm too loyal for my own good."

35

"Maybe—but loyalty is generally a positive trait." What kind of hold did Quincy have over Makayla?

Cal finished talking to Jonas and moved on to a group of girls that circled him. Jonas stood alone, staring into space. I nudged Makayla and motioned toward Jonas. "Do you think he'll talk to me?"

"Let's try." She appeared relieved about the subject change and hurried over to him while I followed. Makayla hugged Jonas. "It'll be okay. Quincy's probably just being Quincy, and she'll turn up in a few days."

"I suppose." He didn't sound convinced. "I can't believe she went to a cemetery in the middle of the night." He shuddered.

"I know, right?" She turned to me. "My stepsister Georgia has assisted the sheriff's department with some tough cases. She's helping us figure out what's going on."

"Really?" Distress lingered in his eyes.

I needed to tell Makayla to stop talking me up, especially when we weren't sure there *was* a case. "I'll do my best to help—if something's wrong."

"Thanks." He twisted a button on his wrinkled shirt. "I don't know much except Quincy wasn't meeting *me* at that cemetery." He glanced over his shoulder. "Don't spread this around, but I have . . . coimetrophobia."

*Oh boy. Do* not *roll your eyes. Do* not *roll your eyes.* "Fear of cemeteries?" I whispered and tried to look sympathetic, even though I was about three seconds away from a giggle attack of epic proportions.

"Yes," he said. "When I was ten, I had to have counseling after my grandma's funeral because I was so freaked out." He looked around again. "I admit Quincy and I don't have the best track record when it comes to sneaking out on chorale tour, but I'm not willing to take that risk any more. I've been working way too hard for my degree to get kicked out of school. I'm graduating in May."

Makayla and I glanced at each other.

"Has Quincy been staying out late with you the last few weeks?" Makayla asked.

"No." He flinched. "Didn't she tell you we broke up?"

"Uh—no. Why were you sitting together on the bus yesterday?" Makayla put her hands on her hips.

His posture stiffened. "Because the breakup was mutual, and we're still friends."

"How long ago did you end things?" I asked.

"About three weeks ago. We decided there was no spark between us anymore. Plus, I'm moving to Nashville after graduation, and Quincy has another year of school."

Jonas's coimetrophobia excuse was too convenient and made me suspect he was hiding something, but it was time to take some heat off him before he shut down. "Was Quincy dating someone else?"

"I don't know. She might've been if she was staying out late." His shoulders relaxed—ever so slightly. "All I know is things were cool between us—as friends."

"Did Quincy ever indicate she was in danger?" I asked.

"No." He shook his head. "Believe me, if I knew something, I'd tell you—and that detective. But I'm thinking this whole thing is Quincy following her own agenda. I care about her, but she can be pretty narcissistic sometimes."

Narcissism would certainly kill a romantic spark.

He looked at Makayla, and then his gaze rested on me. "If I think of something, could I contact you through Makayla?"

"Sure, but first, you should reach out to Detective Perkins," I said. "Thanks for your help, Jonas."

"No problem." He walked away and joined a few guys who were engrossed in a card game.

Makayla and I found an empty pew and people-watched in silence until Sammi approached us a few minutes later. "I have some news." She sat next to Makayla and looked at me. "My cousin Trevor is married to Quincy's oldest sister, Caroline."

"I see." That was a helpful connection.

"I'd forgotten that," Makayla said.

"A few minutes ago, I called Trevor to see if he or Caroline has heard from Quincy. They haven't, and his in-laws are freaking out. Anyway, Trev told me an interesting story." She traced the embroidery on her top. "Back when Quincy was in high school, she dated this older guy who was a musician. She ran away from church camp to be with him and his band for two weeks the summer between her junior and senior years. After the relationship went bad, she came crawling back home."

"Wow," I said.

"I know, right? But it makes me feel better," Sammi said. "Like, this whole thing is just Quincy being Quincy, and she's really okay."

I wasn't convinced *okay* was the right word. "Is that what Trevor and Caroline think?"

"Yeah. Trev said Caroline's super ticked Quincy pulled this stunt again."

Dr. Jackson clapped his hands. "Attention."

The room grew quiet as the students faced Dr. Jackson.

"I'm sure you've heard the unfortunate news that Quincy Ashbrook sneaked out last night and has disappeared. Though she left a note indicating she's fine, we're nonetheless concerned for her safety due to the unexpected nature of her departure. After consulting with university administration and Miss Ashbrook's parents, we've decided to continue with our tour because we have obligations to fulfill. Miss Ashbrook's parents will arrive shortly to assist with the investigation. If any of you know anything about Miss Ashbrook that could be helpful, I encourage you to speak with Detective Perkins immediately, as we will be leaving as soon as the busses are loaded."

Silence throbbed as the students looked around the room, murmuring to each other. Jonas stepped forward. "We need to pray for Quincy—in case something bad happened."

"Yes. Wonderful idea. Thank you," Dr. Jackson said. "Let's form a circle."

The group spread around the pews, and Makayla grabbed my hand and towed me into the formation. Across the room, one of the cute girls who'd gathered around Cal smiled and coaxed him into the circle.

*Great excuse to hold his hand. Nice Georgia.*

Jonas led the prayer, and a few other students chimed in and added petitions for her safety and for her family. When they were finished, the boys began dragging luggage out to the busses in the parking lot while the girls followed behind.

Cal was finally free, so I moseyed over. Something about his early morning visit was bugging me. Though he frequently ran three to four miles at a time, he usually didn't venture all the way out to my farm. "How'd you happen to be running in my neck of the woods?"

He arched an eyebrow. "I'm surprised you haven't heard."

"Are you training for a marathon?"

"I bought Aunt Beverly's house."

# CHAPTER FOUR

N eighbors. Cal and I were going to be neighbors. I grabbed the back of a pew for support and tried hard not to look—How *should* I look? Shocked? Dismayed? Thrilled?

*Merciful heavens.*

I decided on casually interested. "What happened to the other house you were buying?" I asked.

"The inspection showed it had major foundation issues, so I withdrew my offer," Cal said.

Ever since moving to Wildcat Springs from the Cleveland area, he'd wanted a small hobby farm. When we were dating, he'd stopped looking—for a while. Then, out of the blue, he'd put in an offer on a place, just when things were going well between us.

"I'm sure Denise will be glad to keep the house in the family." I forced a smile. "Good for you."

"Thanks."

I twisted my amethyst birthstone ring as silence mocked us.

"Take care." I spun and made a quick getaway to the parking lot where the girls were filing onto the busses and the guys were stowing luggage in the compartments.

Makayla raced over to me. "I'm sorry this happened. Let me know if you hear anything." Tears welled in her eyes as she brushed her wind-whipped hair out of her face.

"Will do. Call if you need me."

She hugged me and boarded the bus. Sammi and Makayla waved as the busses wound through the parking lot and out to the highway.

I zipped my coat and hoofed it to my truck. What a morning, and it wasn't even nine o'clock. I needed a caffeine fix—badly.

---

I hadn't set foot in Latte Conspiracies for several weeks, but it was time to stop avoiding my favorite place. I breathed in the life-giving aroma of freshly brewed coffee as I entered the shop. The Saturday morning crowd occupied the tables scattered next to the exposed brick wall.

On the opposite side of the room, French doors led to a bookstore. The coffee shop's owner, Bobbi Sue Miller, and her sixteen-year-old son Holden worked behind the counter.

Her older son Hamlet was nowhere in sight.

With a sigh of relief, I moved into line and studied the individual clipboard menus that held the drink descriptions and tried to decide between a Crop Circle Cappuccino and a Loch Ness Latte.

I approached the stainless-steel counter and smiled at the middle-aged woman wearing an alien-print T-shirt. Bobbi Sue had always been an excellent source during my past investigations, thanks to her legendary paranoia. "Hey! How's it going?"

She narrowed her eyes. "What do you want?"

Oh boy. I'd been so focused on avoiding Hamlet that I hadn't anticipated his mother's reaction. "Loch Ness Latte please." Why had I thought it was a good idea to get coffee here?

"Large?"

"Yes, please." For the first time ever, I sensed she was judging my higher-than-average coffee consumption. "How was your cruise?" I handed her money and my loyalty card.

Bobbi Sue and her husband had recently traveled to the Caribbean.

"Fine." She shoved my money in the cash register, jammed my loyalty card into the hole punch, and gave it a vigorous squeeze.

Apparently, that's what she wanted to do to my neck, which wasn't entirely fair. I couldn't help it Hamlet had feelings for me —and that until twenty days ago I'd been in a relationship with a man I'd thought I'd marry.

"Hi, Georgia!" Holden grinned and waved from behind the counter.

"Hey!" I moved aside to wait for my drink.

"Hamlet's working on his house today," Holden said. "He's installing bathroom tile."

"Good for him." Hamlet had recently returned home to flip houses after ending his theater career.

"He'd like it if you stopped in."

"I don't think so." Bobbi Sue's eyes flashed as she hovered over her son's shoulder. "You've done enough damage already."

"I—"

"Save your excuses." She put her hands on her hips.

Holden shoved my coffee cup toward me and appeared as if he'd like to teleport to any available location.

*Let me hitch a ride, buddy.*

"Thanks. Have a nice day." I spun toward the door and caught sight of a thin, dark-haired woman sizing me up. Why'd she look familiar? I'd likely seen her around town, but most folks around here at least gave a friendly nod when you made eye contact.

"Oh, no you don't." Bobbi Sue screeched. "Stop right there!"

I jumped and winced as scorching coffee sloshed through the lid hole onto my hand.

Bobbi Sue burst out from behind the counter, and I was firmly convinced that if she'd been younger and more limber, she would've leaped over the counter and tackled me. She blocked my path to freedom. "You're not leaving without a piece of my mind."

*Take it like a woman, Georgia Rae.* I clamped my jaw and met her eyes while trying not to notice the patrons' curious stares.

"Do you know how long I waited for Hamlet to move home?"

*Four, maybe five years?* "No, ma'am."

She scowled. "You don't have any idea what it's like knowing your baby is moving around from place to place. Then he decides to settle down and use those construction skills my dad taught him."

The chattering customers grew quiet. When people had come in for coffee this morning, they hadn't realized they'd be getting a free show as well. My causing two scenes in the span of less than two hours had to be a town record.

She jabbed her pointer finger at me. "Now, because of you, he's moving again."

"He doesn't need to do that. I never asked him to leave. I don't *want* him to move. Besides, I bro—"

"Well, he's got it in his head that he needs to get out of Dodge, and you can't deny it's because of you." She folded her arms across her chest.

No, I couldn't, though to be fair, Hamlet had always known about Cal but had chosen to pursue me anyway. We hadn't even spoken since the night of my grandpa's wedding because Hamlet had been avoiding our Bible study group.

And how on earth had Bobbi Sue not heard that I'd broken up with Cal? She usually knew *everything* that went on in this town. Had people been afraid to mention me in her presence? "I'm sorry."

"I don't want to hear it." She waved a hand and stomped back behind the counter. "You're no longer welcome here."

My stomach somersaulted. For half a second, I wanted to believe Bobbi Sue was messing with me. But her fierce scowl made it clear this was no joke.

With my chin up like the tough Winston I was, I stared straight ahead at the door and marched out of the shop.

---

"Bobbi Sue did *what?*" My other best friend Ashley Choi turned from the cornfield mural she was painting.

I'd walked directly from Latte Conspiracies to Ashley's new art studio and told her what'd happened.

"I'm officially banned." I sipped my final drink from the shop and surveyed the expansive room Ashley was renovating. It spanned the entire second floor of the historic brick building, and tall, narrow windows provided a view onto the streets of downtown Wildcat Springs.

"I'm sorry, hon. Maybe she'll get over it." Ashley pushed her black hair over her shoulder. She wore a pink, oversized button-down shirt adorned with multicolored paint spatters and streaks. She'd recently quit her job as an engineer to open a studio where she'd teach art classes for people of all ages.

I sat on the wood floor and stretched out my legs. "Do you think I should talk to Hamlet?"

Ashley set her paint brush aside and joined me. "Why wouldn't you, hon?" she drawled in her Kentucky accent.

I ran my hand over the woodgrain. "I don't know. I just . . . ."

"You're attracted to him and are afraid of what might happen?" Her dark eyes gleamed.

"Maybe." I took another drink of coffee and set it aside. "I don't know."

I'd never cheated on Cal, but I couldn't deny that there was something I really liked about Hamlet. Or did I simply appreciate he'd never hidden his feelings for me? It was nice to have a guy tell me exactly how he felt. When I'd asked Cal if he loved me, he'd only been willing to admit he cared about me. I pushed away the memory. Whatever the reason for my hesitation, I wasn't ready to dive into another relationship—not when I had unresolved feelings for Cal.

"Look, obviously Hamlet—and his mom—have no idea you and Cal broke up. I can't fathom how they haven't heard, but whatever. And since Hamlet said he was leaving because he didn't want to come between you and Cal, you owe it to the poor guy to tell him what's happening."

"You're right." I'd known it before I'd come to see Ashley. I'd just hoped she'd steer me differently. I drew my knees to my chest.

"You might even decide you want to date him."

"I don't know about that."

"Why?" She grinned. "It doesn't mean you have to marry him."

*Marry him.* I chuckled. "Speaking of marriage. You've *got* to hear about the dream I had last night." I told her about the mystery groom, the horrid dress, and the shooter popping out of the baptistry. "Do you think there's a hidden meaning?"

"Definitely, hon. You're afraid you'll have to settle and marry some random guy to avoid dying alone."

*Life Lesson #11,897: Dying alone is preferable to getting hitched to a guy with a paper bag on his head.* "Maybe subconsciously I'd rather be shot than marry the wrong man."

"That's another possibility."

I traced the frayed hole in my jeans. "I hope it's not a premonition."

"Nah." She waved a hand. "You're still processing everything with Cal. Don't read too much into the dream."

Said the woman who'd just read meaning into my dream.

"How'd it go with the college students last night?" She rubbed a bit of yellow paint off her hand.

I groaned. "Not good." I told her about Quincy stealing my car, disappearing, and Cal showing up at my doorstep. "Even though Quincy left a note, I'm concerned about her, and Makayla is too."

"No kidding. That's crazy." She turned up her sleeves. "Was it weird talking to Cal?"

"A little strained, but I'd better get used to it since he's going to be my neighbor."

"No. Way." Her jaw dropped. "You've had a year's worth of drama in less than twenty-four hours."

I explained that new development. "Anyway. Enough about my issues." I stretched out my legs. "How are things with J.T.?"

She'd recently been on dates with my cousin after he'd had a crush on her for months, though she wasn't ready to commit to a serious relationship after a broken engagement had left her skittish.

"We're having fun hanging out. He's been a big help with the studio." She pointed across the room. "We're going to tackle the restroom reno this weekend."

"That's great, but I thought you didn't want to get into a rela-tionship."

Her cheeks turned a tad pink. "We're taking things slow—and we're on the same page." She studied the wall and got up. "You can stay and talk, but I need to finish this mural." She stood and picked up her paint brush.

I hauled myself off the floor. "I'm going to quit stalling and go talk to Hamlet."

"Good luck with that, hon." She winked.

———

It'd been a month since I'd seen the run-down ranch Hamlet had purchased in the country, and when I parked beside his truck in the driveway, it was clear he'd made progress on the renovation. Though the house's yellowed siding remained, he'd removed the crooked shutters and torn out the box hedges that'd looked like they were devouring the house.

I stepped on the cracked cement porch and knocked on the front door. When he didn't answer, I opened the door, peeked inside, and caught a whiff of joint compound on the newly completed drywall. He was carrying a package of tile across the living room while rocking out to "Layla" by Derek and the Dominoes. His lanky figure danced into the hallway.

I stifled a giggle and hesitated. The last thing I wanted to do was make him drop the tile. I waited a few seconds before going inside.

"Hamlet?" I shouted.

The music stopped, and he entered the living room. "Georgia Rae!" His chiseled face lit up. "This is a surprise." Though he often wore sweater vests, today he had on a blue flannel work shirt, which I liked much better. He'd rolled up the sleeves, displaying the tattoo on his arm—a cross made of nails.

"I need to talk to you." My stomach tightened.

He moved closer. "I apologize for my mother's behavior."

"You've heard?"

"Holden texted me. He enjoys spreading the word."

He'd obviously inherited that trait from their mother. "Thank you for the apology." I studied my silver sneakers. "But I didn't come here because of your mom." I met his blue-gray eyes. He was handsome, and I'd never noticed until he'd moved back to town last month—probably because he was my younger brother's friend. "Are you still planning to leave after you sell this house?"

"Yes. I can make more money in a different market."

"That makes sense, but I don't want you to go because of me."

He walked past me and gazed out the window. "I interfered in your relationship with Detective Perkins, and I'm sorry."

"You already apologized." I wrapped my arms around my waist. "That doesn't mean you have to move."

"We'll inevitably run into each other."

"Our chances are lower now that I've been banned from your mom's shop." I joined him at the window and stared out at the barren field across the road.

"The right thing is to bow out." He smiled ruefully.

"That's very noble, but Cal and I had other problems besides my friendship with you."

He tilted his head. "Had?"

"I broke things off with Cal almost three weeks ago."

His expression remained unchanged. "I see."

Either Hamlet didn't care, which I found hard to believe, or he was using his acting skills. "Please reconsider." I motioned behind me. "You have more work to do on the house, so there's time to make a decision. And there are plenty of houses in Richardville if you want a bigger market."

Outside, stray snowflakes twirled in the wind.

"I'd like to know something, Georgia Rae." He turned and reached for my hand. "Is this visit motivated by guilt, your love of coffee, or the growing attraction between us?" He held my gaze.

My stomach fluttered. Seriously? How did I go from dating a guy who barely talked about his feelings to a man who was willing to throw everything out there? Maybe I preferred the mystery of not knowing where things stood, because even though it was maddening, it was far less scary.

What in the world did that say about me?

"I can buy coffee elsewhere," I said softly.

He moved closer. "Yes, you could." He moved my hand up to his heart.

*Sweet baby Moses in a basket.*

He was going to kiss me. I did *not* come here to be kissed, but I couldn't quite make myself move away. "I've always had an overactive conscience, so yes I suppose you could say that guilt motivates me, but I'd like to think we're friends and that we can live our lives in the same town without making each other feel like we have to—"

*Oh, forget it.*

In the interest of full disclosure, it should be known that I kissed Hamlet, but what was I supposed to do with him standing there looking at me like I was a long-lost treasure?

As soon as our lips met, I couldn't think of anything else, and though I started the whole thing, he took the lead, deepening the kiss and drawing me closer. My entire head swirled, and I'd have dropped right down if I hadn't been holding on.

He broke away and stepped back. "Georgia Rae, we shouldn't do this."

"Why not?" I caught my breath as I sagged against the wall.

"I care too much about you to be your rebound relationship."

"I know." I smoothed my hair. "I'm sorry. I shouldn't have—"

"Don't apologize. I'm simply asking that you give yourself time to heal from your breakup."

"I agree. But will you please reconsider your decision to leave? At the very least, you should be near your family. They missed you."

"Yes, I'll certainly reconsider." He took my hand and squeezed it. "You're probably right about there being some excellent real estate possibilities in Richardville."

I smiled. Mission accomplished—at least for now.

# CHAPTER FIVE

I sped home from Hamlet's house and gazed out at the brown fields on either side of the road. With spring officially here, we were gearing up for planting season, and I hoped the weather would cooperate so the soil would be warm and dry enough for us to get in the field by mid-April.

My *Psych* ringtone broke the silence, and Makayla's name appeared on my truck's navigation screen. *Uh-oh.* I tapped the phone button on my steering wheel.

"Georgia, I need you to come get me." Makayla's quivering voice reverberated through the cab.

"Why?" I squeezed the steering wheel. "Where are you?"

"I can't go on a tour while my friend is missing—even if leaving was her own idea. It's not right. I begged Dr. Jackson to let me off at a rest stop outside of Indianapolis, and he did."

It was official. This had to be one of the weirdest days I'd experienced in years, and it wasn't even noon yet. I eased up on the accelerator as I approached a stop sign. "Is anyone else with you?"

"No." She sniffed. "Most people think Quincy's being selfish, and even I thought so at first, but now I'm not sure. What if she's in danger? I couldn't live with myself if something bad happened."

"I understand. Text me your location. It'll take me at least an hour to get there."

"Okay." Her voice wobbled.

I stopped at the intersection with fields on every corner, and since no other cars were around, I waited for her text. Sure enough, the stop was over an hour away, and I punched the address into my navigation system. Then, I selected Chanticleer from my playlist and let the beautiful music fill my cab as I drove to Indianapolis.

---

After I rescued Makayla at the rest stop, we were both starving, so she found a café that served breakfast and lunch on the city's north side. The cheerful restaurant had Indiana-themed décor with historic pictures and memorabilia from the Colts and Pacers. The hostess seated us in a corner booth with a view of the entire joint.

"My treat." I opened the menu.

"Thanks." Makayla leaned forward. "Will you promise not to tell Dad about me leaving the tour? He's never liked Quincy and thinks she's a bad influence."

I raised my eyebrows. I didn't always agree with mild-mannered Dan, but in this case, he was spot on. "No. You need to tell him. Plus, you should stay with me for the rest of your break —even after the floors are done at Mom and Dan's house."

She fidgeted with the silver charm on her bracelet. "I'm not a kid."

"I get that, but you insisted on leaving your tour because you think Quincy may be in danger and not just gallivanting off to Florida. Right?"

"Maybe."

"I don't feel comfortable with you going home alone. What if Quincy's involved with something shady, and your association with her puts a target on your back?"

"But I don't know anything."

"That you're aware of."

"That's kinda paranoid." She took a sip from her water glass.

"No. It's cautious, and I'm certain your dad would support me." I flipped the menu's pages and stopped at the burgers. "If you don't want to stay with me, you could always stay with Preston or Austin."

She nearly sprayed me with water before she pressed her hand to her mouth and swallowed. "Um. No. Growing up with them was enough."

*That's what I thought.* "Then it's settled. You're my sidekick for the week, and we'll try to figure out why Quincy left—and if she's in trouble."

"Thank you. I'll call Dad later. I'd rather not text about this."

I had a feeling I'd need to make sure she followed through. "I'm getting a bacon cheeseburger with fries." I returned the menu to its holder. "Have you decided?"

"No." She studied the menu.

A few minutes later, a waitress wearing a Pacers T-shirt took our orders, and when she left, Makayla removed her phone from her strawberry-print crossbody and began texting.

"Quincy's mom and dad want to talk to us when they come pick up her things," she said.

"What time?"

"They're in Richardville at the sheriff's department, so later this afternoon. I told them to meet us at your house at 4:00. I hope that's all right."

"Sure." I'd hauled Quincy's suitcase to the church and had forgotten all about it until we'd loaded Makayla's luggage in my truck cab.

She put her phone on the table. "I don't know if I'll be much help since I already told you and Cal everything I know."

I rested my arms on the table. "Earlier you mentioned you were loyal to Quincy, and that's great, but why?"

"Quincy's difficult." Makayla folded the edge of her placemat like an accordion. "It's . . . it's just that I'm not sure if Quincy's a Christian. I mean, she knows *about* Jesus because she was raised to go to church, and her parents are Christians. But I don't see evidence in her life that she understands what it means to follow Christ—not that I'm judging." She looked up. "I feel like God wants me to be an example."

"Do you pray for her?"

"All the time. But I wonder if it's doing any good."

"I understand—and I'll pray for her too."

She took a sip of water. "Thanks."

We people-watched for a few minutes before my phone buzzed. Even though I didn't recognize the number, I answered.

"Georgia, this is Bobbi Sue Miller."

My mind jumped to the memory of kissing Hamlet. What'd gotten into me? I'd never been that aggressive with men in my entire life, which was probably why I was still single in my thirties.

"Hey!" My face grew warm. "What's going on?"

"I apologize for how I acted this morning."

"It's okay. I understand." *But did I?*

"Thank you. Anyway, my son informed me that you asked him to stay in town."

"Yes." I squirmed. What else had he told her? Would she have apologized if I hadn't talked to Hamlet? Had they cranked up the heat in this restaurant? By now I had to look like a tomato, because my stepsister was staring at me with the same look her brothers gave me when they were about to blast off into Let's-Torture-Georgia Mode. I avoided her gaze. "He should be near his family, and he can find some great houses to flip in Richardville."

"I appreciate your efforts with Hammie, so your next drink's on me."

"Thank you, Bobbi Sue." I did a mental happy dance that she'd lifted my ban.

"In fact, stop by this afternoon. I might have some info that'll help you find that girl from Brenneman. You're investigating, right?"

"Yes, ma'am, but we aren't sure if she's even—"

"I heard she stole your car, so I knew you'd look into the case."

"Why don't you tell—"

"See you later this afternoon. Be careful out there."

I disconnected, set my phone on the table, and flipped the edge of my placemat back and forth between my fingers.

"Who's Bobbi Sue?" Makayla asked.

"One of my regular sources who has information to share about Quincy."

She smirked. "Oh, there was *way* more to that conversation than just a tip about Quincy. Who's Hammie, and why do you want him to stay in town?" She waggled her eyebrows.

It'd taken a while, but she'd finally demonstrated that she was truly her brothers' sister. And why, oh why, did I not have the volume turned down on my phone? "*Hamlet* is a friend."

"Interesting name. What kind of friend?"

"Dakota's best buddy from high school." I straightened my fork, knife, and spoon.

"Mmm-hmm. A younger man. Is he handsome?"

"Yes."

"Smart?" She bent forward.

"Very."

"Hard working?"

"Yes."

"Would I be interested?"

I flinched. "No."

She chuckled. "That was a quick answer, but no worries. I'm kidding." She leaned back and crossed her arms. "Is he a good kisser?"

Why in the world would she ask me that? I reached for a menu. "Does this place have milkshakes? I could go for a chocolate one about now." I flipped through the menu and stopped on the page with the desserts.

"He's super good, isn't he?"

I pointed to the menu. "They have lava cake." That sounded even better than a milkshake since I could use a massive dose of chocolate therapy right about now. "I never said I kissed him."

"You didn't have to say a word." She giggled. "Your face already spilled your secret."

I narrowed my eyes. *No dessert for you.*

---

Though I'd attempted to coax Makayla into waiting for Quincy's parents at my house in case they showed up early, she'd insisted on tagging along while I talked to Bobbi Sue.

"Do *not* say anything about Hamlet to Bobbi Sue, or I'm sending you to stay with Preston or Austin." I eased my truck into a space right in front of Latte Conspiracies.

She saluted as she slid out of the truck. "Yes, ma'am."

The bell jingled as we entered the shop. A few patrons sat scattered about while Bobbi Sue was wiping the empty tables.

Makayla walked to the counter and studied the menu. "A

Sasquatch Mocha? This place is awesome," she muttered. "Why have you never brought me here?"

"Georgia!" Bobbi Sue tossed the rag on her shoulder. "Good to see you! What can I make you?"

"If you don't mind, I'll take a raincheck since I'm fully caffeinated for the day." Decaf was a total waste.

"No problem." She turned to Makayla. "How about you, young lady? On the house since you're with Georgia."

"I'd like to try the Sasquatch Mocha, please." Makayla's eyes gleamed.

I made introductions while Bobbi Sue prepared Makayla's drink. "What do you know about the Quincy Ashbrook situation?" I asked.

"First of all, I have to say it's *very* disturbing that the girl abandoned your car at Fillmore Cemetery."

Makayla and I looked at each other. "Why?" I asked.

"You mean to tell me you've lived around the corner from that cemetery most of your life and don't know it's haunted?" She blinked at me, and her tone was completely matter-of-fact.

Makayla drew a sharp breath. "Seriously?"

"That's right." Bobbi Sue poured steamed milk into a paper cup.

I racked my brain and thought I remembered Daddy talking about people believing that. "Now that you mention it, I may've heard something about a phantom dog."

Bobbi Sue slid an alien-print, cardboard ring onto Makayla's cup. "Yep. I could tell you stories about that cemetery from back in my day, but that's for another time." She handed Makayla her mocha.

I loved how Bobbi Sue actually believed the cemetery was haunted. "Let's assume a canine ghost didn't drag her away. What've you heard?"

She flipped the rag off of her shoulder and wiped a smudge

from the counter. "A couple hours after I kicked you out this morning, a man in a Brenneman University jacket came in and asked a bunch of questions."

"What'd he look like?" Makayla asked.

"Oh, my." Bobbi Sue glanced toward the doorway leading to the bookstore that her husband ran, and whispered. "I got the impression he was a professor, and if I were single, he could teach me anything he wanted." She fanned herself. "Tall. Blond. Reminded me of a young Patrick Swayze."

"He was at the concert last night," I said.

Dr. Jackson had blown me off to talk to the man.

"That had to be Dr. Kurtz." Makayla turned to me. "Hold this." She shoved her drink at me and searched on her phone. A minute later she turned it toward Bobbi Sue. "Is this the guy?"

"Sure is." She fanned herself again.

Bobbi Sue's description was right on. Dr. Elias Kurtz's head shot could only be described as smoldering.

I scanned the text beside the picture. "According to his bio, he's a composer, pianist, actor, and health enthusiast."

"He's healthy all right," Bobbi Sue said. "Even though he had on a jacket, you could tell he works out." She patted her biceps.

"Does he teach at Brenneman?" I handed Makayla the cup.

"Yes—he *did*." Makayla took a tentative sip of her drink. "This is good coffee, by the way."

"Thanks." Bobbi Sue beamed. "I'm always thinking of new combinations for my specialty drinks."

I'd try to get Makayla to tell me more about Dr. Kurtz later. Right now, I needed to get all the information I could from Bobbi Sue. "What'd Dr. Kurtz want to know?"

Bobbi Sue glanced around the shop and lowered her voice. "He showed me a picture of a girl he called Quincy and asked me if I'd seen her—because she's *missing*."

# CHAPTER SIX

"Dr. Kurtz used the words 'she's missing'?" I asked.

"Sure did," Bobbi Sue said. "Seemed odd, especially since Ruby Daniels was in here telling me how she was at church this morning and overheard Dr. Jackson say he thought Quincy ran off on her own—and that your ex-boyfriend had done some investigating and was thinking the same thing. Something about Quincy leaving a note?"

"She did." I figured there was no harm in confirming what was common knowledge. "We found it in my car." It was probably best not to mention she'd ditched her ID and credit cards.

"I knew something wasn't right." Makayla gripped her coffee cup with both hands.

"What else did Dr. Kurtz say?" I asked.

"He had some questions about local law enforcement and how effective they are. Of course, I gave him my honest opinion," Bobbi Sue said.

Makayla glanced at me. "Which is?"

*Oh, boy.* I steeled my face—and that was no easy task.

"Tell you what." Bobbi Sue pressed both hands onto the

counter and leveled her gaze at Makayla. "Things have improved a lot since I was your age, but I still don't trust cops—never have. Never will. Now I like that detective she used to date." She pointed at me. "But I'd only trust him so much, if you know what I mean."

"I think so?" Confusion flitted over Makayla's face.

"Anyhow. Dr. Kurtz seemed worried, and if you want my opinion, he was more concerned about Quincy than the average professor should be." Bobbi Sue raised her eyebrows. "Especially since the picture was a selfie of them cozying up on a couch."

Interesting. Had Quincy been staying out late with Dr. Kurtz?

As usual, Bobbi Sue had provided great information, but we needed to scoot if we were going to make it home in time to meet Quincy's parents. "Thanks for your help."

"Any time. Again, I'm sorry for kicking you out this morning." She grinned sheepishly.

Once we were in my truck, I turned to Makayla.

"Spill," we said in unison.

"Hold the phone." I buckled my seatbelt. "What am *I* spilling?"

"Duh. Why'd Bobbi Sue kick you out?"

I weighed my options. If I was going to have any chance at finding Quincy, then I needed Makayla to be completely honest about Elias Kurtz—and anything else that might be helpful. There was probably zero chance of her doing that if I didn't tell her about this morning's incident.

"Okay." I told the story of Hamlet pursuing me and ended with an explanation of Bobbi Sue kicking me out of her shop and my trip to Hamlet's house to ask him to stay.

"And that's when you kissed him."

"I never said that." I started my truck.

"We've been over this. I know you kissed him, so you might as well admit it."

"Ugh!" I threw my hands up. "You're right. I did, but he looked like he was going to kiss me first." I eased my truck into traffic and drove down Main Street past Velda's Café and the post office.

"Your life is way more interesting than I thought."

"Thanks." It took every ounce of strength I possessed not to roll my eyes. "Now. My turn. You were holding back about Dr. Kurtz, and I don't blame you. It's not smart to tell Bobbi Sue everything you know."

"Remember that when she's your mother-in-law someday."

I coughed. "Whoa, let's back that train up." Wildcat Springs disappeared behind us as I sped down the country road toward my house. "I'm not sure Hamlet and I are even going to date."

"Because you're not over Cal?"

"Something like that."

"I'm not sure he's over you."

"Why?" I kept my eyes fixed on the road.

"It's obvious he still cares about you. He looked so worried this morning."

"You think?" I'd thought the same thing but didn't want to get my hopes up.

"Yep. The plot thickens." She displayed jazz hands. "*Hamlet Versus Cal—The Musical*. Coming to Wildcat Springs in March 20—"

"Tell me everything you know about Dr. Kurtz and Quincy." I dodged a pothole and choked back a laugh at the mental image of Cal breaking into a song and dance—though it certainly wasn't a stretch to picture Hamlet doing that very thing.

"Nice subject change." She grinned. "I took voice lessons from Dr. Kurtz my freshman year, and rumor has it he was quite a ladies' man. He never came on to me, but Quincy said he made a pass at her."

"Did she mind?"

She shook her head. "Definitely not. She was giddy, even though she was dating Jonas. You saw Dr. Kurtz's picture, right? But if she was secretly involved with him, she never told me. Anyway, he didn't come back to teach at Brenneman this year. I heard he decided to pursue a musical theater career."

"If he wasn't a faculty member, he'd be free to have a relationship with Quincy. Maybe she's been staying out late with *him*."

"I doubt it. She would've bragged about being with him."

I wasn't so sure. "See if you can figure out where he's working."

"Sure."

I turned into my driveway. Cal had taken care of returning Gretel Grand Prix and had parked the car next to the garage.

"Got it." Makayla held her phone so I could see. "Dr. Kurtz has been cast as Captain VonTrapp in the *Sound of Music*—at Bell's Dinner Theater in Richardville."

We got out of the truck.

"When does the show open?"

"Tonight."

"He hasn't been busy with performances, but maybe they've had evening rehearsals. Quincy could've been meeting up with him afterward, which might explain why she was late." I unlocked the back door.

"Makes sense."

I hung my keys on the holder. "It bugs me how Dr. Kurtz knew about her disappearance so quickly. If he doesn't work for the school, then who told him?" I dropped my purse onto the kitchen table while Gus went crazy barking in his crate.

"He might've heard from Dr. Jackson." Makayla kicked off her ankle booties.

"But why?"

She shrugged. "They're friends? Dr. Kurtz was at our concert last night."

"Maybe." As I freed Gus, I hoped she was right, because if she wasn't, then Elias Kurtz most likely had something to do with Quincy disappearing and was trying to cover his tracks.

---

"Thank you for agreeing to talk with us about Quincy." Stuart Ashbrook crossed my living room as his attractive, slender wife Janet hovered beside him.

"We're happy to help." I guessed they were both in their mid-fifties.

"We had no idea when we asked to talk to Makayla that her stepsister is a detective." He straightened his broad shoulders, unbuttoned his navy sport coat, and sat stiffly on the edge of my sectional sofa.

Still needed to chat about that with Makayla. "I'm really more of—"

"We came from the sheriff's department, and the detectives weren't helpful at all." Janet dabbed her eyes with a wadded tissue and leaned against her husband.

I settled in my daddy's old recliner. "Did you file a missing person report?"

"Yes. But that hotshot male detective told us there wasn't any evidence that Quincy is in danger, and she'll probably turn up in a few days. That's unacceptable!" His voice boomed as he curled his fingers into a fist. "We can't wait a few days!"

Janet rested her hand on his knee. "He did say they'd look into the matter further."

"He didn't appear motivated." Stuart snarled.

I shifted. *Don't get defensive. Don't get defensive.*

"Not to mention it's unbelievable that Dr. Jackson continued with this tour when my daughter is missing. I'll be going above his head with my complaints!"

Makayla clutched a throw pillow to her chest and looked as if she wished the couch would swallow her.

Janet turned toward her husband. "Let's deal with our grievances later, dear. We don't need to unload on these girls who've been kind enough to offer help."

His square jaw twitched as if he wanted to say more but was holding back to help keep up appearances.

"Our daughter *loves* singing." Janet fingered her diamond pendant. "She'd never, ever blow off a tour. Chorale means too much to her."

Quincy hadn't given *me* that impression, but I'd go along with Janet. "Could Quincy have had a good reason to leave even though chorale is important? Her note mentioned there was something she had to take care of."

"Oh, no. We raised her to be considerate and responsible. Once you make a commitment, you follow through. It's how our family operates," Janet said. "I can't fathom a single instance where she'd behave like this on purpose."

I sneaked a sideways glance at Makayla, and her intense concentration could've earned her a PhD in hangnail picking. Given what Sammi had told us about Quincy running away in high school, I was right there with my stepsister.

I cleared my throat. "Did Quincy run off with a band when she was in high school?"

Stuart glared at me. "Where did you hear that?"

"So it's not true?" I held his gaze.

"It's true," Janet said. "Quincy has matured and regrets how she made us feel during that awful time. She wouldn't put us through an ordeal like that again. Nevertheless, as a precaution, we've already contacted the young man she ran away

MARISSA SHROCK

with. He's in medical school in California and hasn't heard from Quincy in years. I'm telling you." She slammed her hand against her leg in time with her words. "Someone coerced her into writing that note and kidnapped her!" Her tears spilled over.

"I'm sorry for upsetting you, but it's helpful to have accurate information." I opened my end table drawer, removed a package of tissues, and passed them to Janet. "Are you anticipating a ransom demand?"

"No." Stuart said. "We're comfortable but don't have a fortune hidden away. We don't even have wealthy relatives."

"Would your jobs give you access to information that would be appealing to a kidnapper?" I looked back and forth between them.

"I've been blessed to stay at home since our children were born, and before that I taught elementary music in a private school." Janet dabbed her eyes.

Stuart patted his wife's leg. "She also volunteers at the music camp ministry our church runs—Camp Winland. I worked in the life insurance industry for over thirty years and retired six months ago."

"We're terrified that she's been trafficked." Fresh tears welled in Janet's eyes, and she reached for her husband's hand.

I wished I could reassure her that things like that didn't happen in rural Indiana, but I knew better—human trafficking was everywhere.

Stuart clenched his fist. "These rural sheriff's departments are incredibly incompetent. Before we left, I told them if something happens to my daughter, they'll be hearing from my lawyer."

Annnddd . . . we were back to that dead horse. I took a deep breath. "I'm sorry for your difficulty with the sheriff's department. That must make a stressful situation worse." I deserved an

A+ for how soothing I sounded. "We'll be praying for Quincy's safe return."

"Thank you." Janet leaned forward and adjusted her navy cardigan, which was the exact shade of her husband's sport coat.

Had they coordinated outfits on purpose?

"Did you notice anything strange when Quincy was here?" Janet turned her teary face toward Makayla. "Or in the weeks before she . . ." She ducked her head and swiped her cheeks.

Makayla twisted her hands. "We weren't talking that much recently—"

"Did you have a fight?" Stuart narrowed his eyes.

"No," Makayla said. "We've been busy this semester, and I've got a heavy class load since I changed my major."

"But surely you saw each other in the evenings," Janet said.

"Quincy was gone a lot." Makayla avoided looking at her friend's parents.

"What do you mean she was gone?" Stuart's posture somehow grew even more rigid. "Was she at the music building? Was she working?"

"All I know was that she was staying out late."

"What kind of roommate are you? If there's something you're hiding to protect Quincy, you need to stop." Stuart raised his voice. "Or are you defending yourself, because you've been a negative influence on my daughter?"

I bristled. "Sir, if you continue speaking to Makayla using that tone, this conversation is over."

"It's over when I say it's over, and I'll use whatever tone I want." Stuart's eyes blazed, and he looked like he was about to lunge off the couch and tackle me—or beat me senseless.

Janet squeezed his arm.

I gritted my teeth.

"She may have a new boyfriend," Makayla blurted.

Quincy's parents exchanged glances.

Janet's eyes widened. "What about Jonas?"

"He told us this morning that he and Quincy broke up a couple of weeks ago," I said.

Janet removed a fresh tissue from the pack and dabbed her red nose. "She never shared that with me."

There was the shock of the century. "Did Quincy ever mention Elias Kurtz?"

"The name sounds familiar." Stuart tilted his head and looked at his wife.

Janet turned to her husband. "Remember, his mother Sylvia was in my class at Brenneman. We spoke at our reunion and figured out the connection. We all thought it was so neat he was Q's voice instructor freshman year."

"That's right." Stuart said.

I didn't dare look at Makayla. "Did Elias keep in touch with Quincy after he left Brenneman?"

"Not that I know of." Janet stared at me as if she were trying to figure out how that information could possibly be relevant.

"Hold on." His expression darkened. "Why all the questions about Elias Kurtz?"

This was quickly turning into a minefield. "Elias came to Wildcat Springs and asked the owner at the local coffee shop some questions about Quincy after he heard she's missing."

"Why would he do that?" Confusion flickered in Janet's expression.

I folded my hands in my lap as awkward silence invaded the room.

Then, his eyes flashed. "Are you suggesting my daughter is having a fling with Elias, and *that's* why she's been staying out at all hours?"

"I have no idea." I shifted. "But Dr. Kurtz was asking questions about your daughter. Not to mention, he had a picture of them together."

"Fine. But that doesn't mean she was seeing him. He was her professor." Janet's firm tone and accusatory expression matched her husband's. "Quincy would *never* have an inappropriate relationship. We gave her a purity ring when she was thirteen."

If only purity rings came with a protective forcefield. *Do not laugh, Georgia Rae.* I'd heard Brandi talk about students' parents who never believed their children misbehaved or made bad choices. But experiencing it was a whole different story.

"How do we know you and Makayla didn't have anything to do with her taking off?" Stuart stood. "You're trying to distract us with this ridiculous accusation about my daughter. I think you saw an opportunity to sell an innocent young girl to a pimp."

My jaw dropped, and Makayla gasped. I had a passing thought of releasing Gus from his crate. Though he was far from ferocious, his friendly—and hairy—greeting would probably be enough to freak out Mr. and Mrs. Perfect.

But he'd probably just sue me.

"Maybe your crops didn't do well, and you needed some cash to save the family farm." Stuart looked around my home with disgust. "Perhaps you even think you can get law enforcement to look the other way, since you've helped them in the past. A little quid pro quo." He pointed at me. "Don't think I won't hire a PI to check your background."

With my face burning, I stood. "You're certainly within your rights to take whatever measures you feel are necessary to find your daughter, and you're welcome to check my background. I have nothing to hide." I met his gaze. "But this conversation is over, and you need to leave my house."

Stuart and his wife made their way to my front door, and he grabbed Quincy's suitcase.

Janet stopped and shot me a mournful look before turning to Makayla. "If you think of anything—even the smallest detail— please promise you'll let the detectives know."

"I will," she said. "And we'll be praying for Quincy to make it home safely."

"Thank you." Janet took her husband's arm and walked down my sidewalk.

I closed the door and sagged against it. "Wow."

"I know, right? I'm so sorry."

"It's not your fault."

"Yet somehow, I still feel responsible since I told them they could come."

"It's okay. They're just worried." And a little unhinged.

She twisted her bracelet. "Now what?"

I took a deep breath. "First, I'm going to call Cal and tell him everything that's happened today—just in case this turns into a big investigation."

"Then?"

"Are you up for *The Sound of Music* tonight?"

---

While Makayla was getting ready for our trip to Bell's Dinner Theater, I shuffled through my closet choosing an outfit and waiting for Cal to answer his phone. I was trying not to admit that a part of me was thrilled I had a legitimate excuse to talk to him. After all, he needed to know about Elias Kurtz nosing around, and Bobbi Sue couldn't be counted on to initiate a conversation with a cop.

And it wouldn't hurt for him to know that the Ashbrooks thought I was guilty of human trafficking.

"Cal's phone." Cigarettes had honed the woman's voice into a friendly rasp.

I froze with my hand on a black pencil skirt. Did Cal have a new girlfriend already? What about Taryn?

"What can I do for you, Georgia?"

"I'll call back later." I pushed the pencil skirt aside and withdrew a red jersey dress.

"You sure? Because Cal stepped out to let his dog pee and should be back in a sec. I tell you, I nearly hit the floor when I heard he'd adopted Miss Peacock. I could never get him to take responsibility for our mutt when he was a kid. He got that trait from his dad. It was always me feeding and taking Mindy out."

I nearly dropped my phone. "Mrs. Perkins?" I tossed the dress on my bed.

"It's *Ms. Conner* now—but you can call me Yvonne. Took my maiden name back in the divorce. My boyfriend and I are thinking about tying the knot someday, but Yvonne's not changing her last name again. Too much work." She emitted a cackle-croak.

*A croakle.*

"I see. Please tell Cal I have some information about the Quincy Ashbrook case, and he can call me back at his—"

"You've met my ex, so I'm sure you understand why I don't want to be saddled with his name."

I'd tried to block out the memory of Darrell Perkins but hadn't been successful. "We met when he came for Beverly's funer—"

"I heard. I hope you didn't end things with Cal because of Darrell and his big mouth, but I wouldn't blame you if you did. You marry a man, you marry his family. Anyway, you got information about Quincy Ashbrook, huh? Cal told me her parents threatened to sue. From what he told me, if that pair had raised me, I'd vanish too." She croakled again. "I dealt with a lot of entitled people back when I—"

"Mom, who is that?"

"Your ex-girlfriend. Nice talking to you, Georgia. I hope we can meet while I'm here in town. In fact, I might stroll down the road to your place and say—"

"Hey, Georgia." He lowered his voice. "And I'm sorry."

I let out a giggle that was a twenty out of ten on the dorkiness scale. "It's okay." At least she hadn't accosted me like Bobbi Sue—and Yvonne would've had many more reasons to chew me out. "I wanted to let you know a few things I learned today." I updated him on Bobbi Sue's information and the Ashbrooks' visit. When I finished, he chuckled.

"I can't believe they think you sold Quincy to a pimp."

I pictured his dimple, and my heart fluttered. "I don't know how I get in such messes."

"I've never seen anything like it."

Did I hear a teeny-tiny note of affection in his tone? Or was it my overactive imagination?

He cleared his throat. "Anyway, thanks for passing along the information."

I wound a strand of hair around my finger. "It's nice your mom's visiting." It wouldn't hurt to sneak in a mini fishing expedition before the conversation sputtered out.

"She wanted to see my new house and help me get settled."

"Cool." On second thought, I'd better cut this conversation short before it took a wrong turn into awkward territory. "I'll let you know if I hear anything else about Quincy."

"Thanks. Take care."

After disconnecting, I closed my eyes and tried to convince myself I didn't miss him.

My valiant effort failed.

# CHAPTER SEVEN

W alking into Bell's Dinner Theater in Richardville with Makayla, I tried to push away the memory of the last time I'd been here to see *Grease*—with Cal. Though it wasn't a romantic outing because Detective Vanessa Hawk and her fiancé Curtis had joined us for a double date, the memory still stabbed my heart.

I hadn't been able to get the best seats because of our last-minute decision to attend *The Sound of Music*, but I snagged decent tickets that included a meet and greet with the cast at the conclusion of the play. That'd cost me an extra twenty bucks, but it would give us easy access to Elias Kurtz.

We found our seats in the back row of the U-shaped theater. Buffet stations were arranged on the stage below and would be removed before the show.

"This place is super cool," Makayla said. She was wearing a black polka-dot dress with a contrasting lacy white collar, and the vintage vibe fit with the musical's era.

"You've never been here?"

"No. Dad and the boys are all about sports. Mom was too. I'm the family weirdo since I'm into music."

"I'm glad we're here then."

"Me too." She put her napkin in her lap.

After a waitress dressed as a nun took our drink orders, we gorged at the buffet, which included schnitzel with noodles. The show began, and at intermission, we found room for apple strudel.

When the show was over, the waitress-nun led us backstage to the greenroom where Elias Kurtz waited with the actors and actresses who'd played Maria and the children. Makayla and I complimented the kids and Maria on their performances, and when we reached Elias, he smiled broadly.

"Makayla Farthing." He extended both hands. "Nice to see you again. Are you still singing?"

"Yes." She clasped his hands. "You're a fantastic Captain VonTrapp. Even though I'm from Richardville, this is my first experience at Bell's, and I loved it." She batted her eyes and gazed at him.

*You go, girl.*

"I'm glad." He gave me the once over and dropped Makayla's hands. "Who's your friend?"

"My stepsister Georgia."

Ignoring the feeling that I needed a shower, I shook his hand.

Makayla flipped her hair over her shoulder. "Have you heard about Quincy Ashbrook's disappearance? I know she took voice lessons from you too."

Would I even be needed here? I felt a burst of pride at my stepsister's investigative-flirting skills.

"No. What happened?" His eyes widened.

So that's how he was going to play it. Interesting choice.

"Quincy, Sammi Cardwell, and I were staying with Georgia after our first concert on chorale tour," Makayla said. "Quincy stole Georgia's car in the middle of the night. A cop found it abandoned this morning at a cemetery, but she left a note saying she had something to take care of and she'd be back after spring break is over."

His mouth dropped open. "That's strange. I hope she's okay."

I gave my eyes stern orders not to roll. For a guy who'd just given a commendable performance as Captain VonTrapp, he sure was botching this act.

"Me too," Makayla said.

I couldn't take any more of his charade. "Dr. Kurtz. The show's over. We know you were in Wildcat Springs earlier today asking questions about Quincy and showing a picture of the two of you together." I stared until he looked away. "How about being honest with us."

Red crept up his neck, and he glanced around the room. "Could we wait until this meet-and-greet is over and talk in private?" he whispered.

"Where do you want to have this discussion?" I crossed my arms.

His gaze flicked toward the exit. "My dressing room. Give me ten minutes."

"Fine." We moved away so other audience members could gush over his performance as he signed programs and headshots. "I'm not letting him out of my sight until he talks to us," I muttered.

"Good call," Makayla whispered.

Fifteen minutes later, the room had cleared, and Dr. Kurtz escorted us down a narrow hallway. The woman who'd played Maria had changed into a Fitness Universe Staff sweatshirt and was on her way out the back exit. She glared as we passed. He opened a door with his name on it, snapped on the lights, and stepped aside so we could enter.

"Have a seat." He motioned to a green velvet couch pushed against a wall with gold hexagonal print wallpaper.

I perched on the edge of the couch, and Makayla's posture mimicked mine.

He scooted a chair away from his lighted makeup counter, turned it toward us, and straddled it. "Thanks for waiting. And feel free to call me Elias."

That wasn't going to happen—at least to his face—because I didn't like his overly familiar tone. "I'll get right to the point. Why were you in Wildcat Springs asking questions about Quincy?"

He stared at the worn carpet. "I know it looks like I'm more than her former voice teacher."

"Yes," I said.

"But I can explain." Elias jiggled his leg. "I'm a distributor for Tune Nutritional Supplements, and Quincy's part of my downline."

# CHAPTER EIGHT

Quincy being part of Elias's downline in a multi-level marketing company seemed like a convenient excuse to cover up a forbidden romantic relationship, but I decided to go along with him for the moment. "How long has Quincy been selling?"

"A couple of years—since she was a freshman. We took the picture you mentioned after she joined my team." He turned to his makeup table, lifted a business card from a holder sitting next to his cellphone, and handed it to me. "Our vitamins help people keep their bodies in tune."

I studied the card emblazoned with his name, phone number, and the Tune Nutritional Supplement Logo before handing it to Makayla, who appeared puzzled.

"How'd you get her started?" I asked Elias.

"Quincy saw my water bottle with the company logo and asked about it during a voice lesson." He tugged the skin under his neck. "She decided to try her hand at selling, and for a while, she made a lot of money from online sales, but she hasn't been very active lately."

Interesting. My eyes fell on Elias's phone, and a theory about why Quincy had abandoned her phone formed in my mind. "Does she happen to have a second phone for business?" I asked.

Now his leg jostled in double time. "Not that I know of. Why?"

"She left her phone behind at my house, and I can't imagine she'd want to be cut off from her customers—or anyone else."

His leg froze in mid jiggle. "Wow. That's weird. I can't picture her without it." There was no mistaking the concern in his voice.

"Can you think of any reason why Quincy would vanish without her credit cards?" Makayla asked.

"Perhaps she didn't want to be tempted to use them. She mentioned having debt." He studied his hands. "Or . . . I do know her parents pressured her to succeed. Maybe it got too overwhelming, and she decided to leave everything behind and start over."

"Did you ever hear her talk about running away?" I asked.

"A while back, she joked about escaping to a deserted island —but it's something you say when you're upset. I didn't take her seriously, especially since she'd admitted to having a fight with her boyfriend."

That seemed like a pretty personal thing to share with a voice professor, which meant it was time for the big question. "Have you ever had a romantic relationship with Quincy?"

The red that had made an appearance in his neck earlier made a vicious comeback. "No, I think of her as a little sister."

"Why'd you leave Brenneman?" I asked.

He curled his fingers into a fist. "The university chose not to renew my contract. They never gave a reason other than I wasn't a good fit—and they didn't have to because I wasn't tenured. It didn't help that Dr. Jackson—the music department head—had it out for me."

"Do you know why?" I asked.

"He couldn't stand that I was more popular with the students than him. He even resented me being at the concert last night. He strolled by and gave me a curt 'hello' and a scowl." Elias performed a perfect impression of the stuffy professor.

I'd have to ask Makayla about Elias's popularity later, but there was another question that'd been bugging me. "Dr. Kurtz, who told you Quincy ran away?" I was becoming more and more certain Elias was lying about his relationship with Quincy—and the reason his contract hadn't been renewed.

Elias's face darkened. "Gresham—Dr. Jackson—called this morning and asked if I knew anything about Quincy. I told him I didn't talk to her last night, and I haven't heard from her for a while—probably because her sales have tanked."

"Why would Dr. Jackson contact you?" I met his gaze.

"He buys Tune from me and knows Quincy's part of my team." He rested his head in his hand. "After I heard from Gresham, I was worried and thought the least I could do is go to Wildcat Springs and ask a few questions." He briefly closed his eyes. "I just can't stand the thought of something bad happening to her."

---

"Elias was definitely lying about his relationship with Quincy," I said as soon as Makayla and I were back in my truck and on our way home from Richardville.

"No way."

I stopped for a red light and searched Makayla's face for a hint of sarcasm. Nothing. Nada. Zilch. "Okaayy. Why do you think he was telling the truth?"

"Because I do."

"That's not a reason."

"Dr. Kurtz wouldn't lie."

"How do you know?"

"How do *you* know he *was?*" She glared at me. "You're not a human lie detector."

I smothered a sigh. "His body language indicated he was hiding something. Plus, you told me he made a pass at Quincy, and she was giddy about it." The light changed, and I eased through the intersection. "But you know him better than I do, so I'll listen to your reasoning. Convince me why I'm wrong." We continued past a row of fast-food restaurants.

"I'd know if my roommate was seeing him."

"You told her parents—and me—you didn't know where she was going at night."

She huffed. "She would've told me about Dr. Kurtz."

"Even if he was seeing her while he was working at Brenneman, and their relationship meant he'd lose his job if someone found out?"

"But he's not working there anymore, so she'd be free to tell." She crossed her arms. "I just don't think he's lying. Remember I was right when I said Dr. Kurtz heard about Quincy from Dr. Jackson."

"You thought it was because they're friends—and they aren't."

"Whatever." She reached out and changed the satellite radio to a 1980s station playing "Silent Running" by Mike and the Mechanics.

I used the steering wheel buttons to turn down the volume.

"My mom liked this song." She turned up the volume and sang along.

I let her go because I wasn't going to mess with the mom card. Still, it wasn't a good sign that Makayla felt the need to defend Elias. She could sing all she wanted, but she was only delaying the inevitable question from me.

The song ended, and I jabbed the radio's power button. "I need you to be straight with me about something."

"Fine."

"Was Elias ever more than a professor to *you*?" I set my jaw.

"No."

"Are you *sure*? Because if you're not going to be honest, this investigation ends now, and you can go stay with one of your brothers." I peeked at her out of the corner of my eye.

She gazed out the window. "I may have a little crush that's influencing my judgment. But Dr. Kurtz always acted professional with me. I loved taking lessons from him, and I was sad when he didn't come back this year." Her tone had lost the defensive edge. "That's it."

"Okay. We'll give him the benefit of the doubt and look at other angles." *For now.* I glanced in the rearview mirror. "Was Elias more popular than Dr. Jackson?"

"Yes. Dr. Jackson's nice, but he's super stuffy. Dr. Kurtz is ten times more personable—and approachable. I can see why Dr. Jackson felt threatened."

"But their feud doesn't help us know what happened to Quincy." I tapped my fingers against the steering wheel. "When did she start dating Jonas?"

"They got together after a pick-a-date the fall of our freshman year. He was a sophomore."

"What's a pick-a-date?"

"What it sounds like. Someone in your dorm plans a big group activity, and you ask a guy to be your date. Freshman year, our floor did a murder mystery dinner. Quincy had hit it off with Jonas, so she chose him."

"And you?"

Makayla sighed. "I asked Jonas's friend Micah because Quincy and I thought the guys could stick together if it didn't go well." She wrinkled her nose. "It did. For Quincy and Jonas.

Micah is a nice guy, but I couldn't get past his 1980s aviator glasses."

"But you like vintage."

"That's one trend that needs to stay dead." She gagged.

"Amen. Is Micah in chorale?"

"No, but he's in a band with Jonas." She smoothed her skirt. "Speaking of Jonas. You know something weird that I hadn't realized until tonight?"

"What's that?"

"Quincy's been selling Tune supplements since freshman year, but I always thought Jonas recruited her—I had no idea it was Dr. Kurtz."

"Is that what she told you?"

"No. I just assumed since Jonas sells it too. I never asked a lot of questions, and she didn't bug me after I wouldn't buy."

We rode a few miles in silence.

"Would you be willing to take me to Brenneman tomorrow after church so I can get my car?" Makayla asked.

"You mean you don't want me to chauffer you around for the next week?"

"Um, no. But I was also thinking I could look around our room to see if Quincy left any clues."

I smothered a grin. "That trip could be arranged as long as you keep your promise to be honest with me."

"No problem. You're way more fun than I realized."

*Gee. Thanks.*

# CHAPTER NINE

Sunday morning, I was pouring a cup of coffee when Makayla shuffled into the kitchen.

"They cancelled the chorale tour." She yawned and pointed to her phone. "Sammi texted late last night, but I didn't see it until I woke up."

Gus walked over and rubbed his nose against her hibiscus-print pajama bottoms.

I dumped some creamer into my owl mug and stirred. "Did she give any other details?" I had a pretty good idea Stuart Ashbrook was behind the change of plans.

"University administration decided it was in the best interest out of respect for Quincy's family." She patted Gus's head. "Which, roughly translated means, 'We don't want to tick off one of our rich donors.'"

I tossed my spoon in the sink. "Quincy's parents implied they're not wealthy."

"Mr. Ashbrook said they're *comfortable*." She made air quotes. "Don't you know that's rich-people code for loaded?"

"A lot of people might say that about our family."

"Sure. Dad does well, but Quincy's family is on a whole other level. They have a live-in maid, and they take fancy vacations. Quincy drives a BMW." She shook her head as worry settled in her expression. "Cancelling a tour affects a lot of people, so this is a huge deal. Do you think the school administration knows something we don't?"

I wanted to say something reassuring, but I couldn't quite get there. "I sure hope not."

---

As Pastor Mark began his sermon, I scanned the congregation at Wildcat Springs Community Church, and my gaze fell on Hamlet, sitting one section over. Our eyes met, and I waved—as discreetly as possible.

Makayla scribbled *Hamlet?* on her bulletin and shoved in front of me.

I nodded. He'd chosen a pale-yellow sweater vest from his vast collection. At least the color reminded me of springtime. If we dated, would I be able to steer him away from his sweater-vest habit? Or did I care? *Nah.* Hamlet was Hamlet, and I'd have to accept his quirkiness.

And what about Cal? The concern in his eyes yesterday morning had me wishing I'd given him more time to open up about what'd been troubling him. Would that have made a difference, since he couldn't tell me he loved me? Besides, he was with Taryn now, so it was too late.

Makayla elbowed me. "Pay attention," she whispered.

My cheeks warmed. At least she didn't make kissing noises, like her brothers would've. "Sorry," I mumbled.

"Don't apologize to me." She rolled her eyes toward the heavens, opened my Bible, and pointed to Psalm 42.

I stifled a giggle and turned to the sermon outline in my

bulletin. The title was "Praising God through Our Difficulties." Yeah. I should be paying attention all right.

" . . . something happens when we worship God," Pastor Mark said. "That doesn't mean we have to praise him for our terrible circumstances, but we praise God for being the one who loves us and will never forsake us in circumstances we don't understand."

I glanced at my Bible, and my eyes fell on verse eleven of Psalm 42.

*Why, my soul, are you downcast? Why so disturbed within me? Put your hope in God, for I will yet praise him, my Savior and my God.*

I clicked a pen and underlined the verse. The message from the scripture was clear. Even if the state of my love life disturbed and confused me, I needed to put my hope in God and praise him —no matter what.

———

After church, Makayla and I grabbed sandwiches at Velda's Café and then drove an hour east to Brenneman University. A stately brick sign beckoned us onto the campus, and I circled the winding drive past dorms and academic buildings. A large, white chapel stood in the middle of the campus, surrounded by a prayer garden with a water feature made of boulders.

Makayla directed me to a three-story dorm with large white columns and *McKibben* in black letters over the main entrance. I parked on the street in front of the building.

"So, here's the thing," Makayla said.

I didn't like her cagey tone. "What?"

"Technically, the dorm is closed because it's spring break. Sammi told me they weren't even allowed to stay in their rooms last night. They were assigned to professors' houses and were briefly allowed in this morning to get stuff for the rest of break."

"I drove all the way over here, and we can't get in." Was this what it felt like to be a parent?

She displayed her ID. "I'll try swiping my card, but we may have to go to the campus security office and beg." She leaped out and ran to the door while I lingered behind.

This felt shady, but I'd done plenty of questionable things in my quest for answers during investigations.

Makayla swiped her card, and the light on the keypad remained red. She tried again, and when that didn't work, she faced me. "On to the campus security office." She pointed at my truck.

"We should've gone there first," I muttered and fished my keys from my pocket.

"But I wanted to see if the residence directors were telling the truth about restricting our access or if they were bluffing."

I laughed as I got in the truck. "Did you and your brothers get this trait from your mom?"

"What trait?"

"The pushing-boundaries trait. Because I don't see that quality in Dan—at all." He was a buttoned-up lawyer who spent his days combing through contracts.

"For sure. Mom was always playing pranks and cracking jokes. Not to be rude, but it surprised me when Dad married Jill —because she's more serious. Even though she's nice."

My mom was a librarian, and though she had a good sense of humor, my dad had been the ornery one in their relationship. "It works for them."

"Yeah. Follow this road around until you come to that lime-stone building ahead."

I parked in the lot next to the squat building, and we hurried inside where a young man with a buzz cut greeted us. I put him at about twenty-five.

"What can I do for you?" he asked.

"I'm Makayla Farthing." She flashed her ID. "I live in McKibben Hall—room 318."

He typed something and studied his computer screen. "I see you live with the Ashbrook girl who went missing."

I rested my hand on Makayla's shoulder and feigned shock. "Last we knew, Quincy appeared to have left on her own. Has there been a new development?"

He stood—and he was shorter than both Makayla and me. "I don't know details—just rumors." He glanced back and forth between us. "How can I help?"

"My spring break plans changed, and I need access to my room to get my car keys," Makayla said. "Will you let my step-sister and me in?"

He lifted his chin. "Well, I don't know if I ought to, given the circumstances."

"What circumstances?" I wanted him to explain his reasoning.

"The Ashbrook girl." He looked as if he were dying to tack a *duh* onto that statement.

"If there haven't been any new developments with Quincy, then I don't understand the problem—especially if you accompany us. Weren't the chorale members allowed into their rooms this morning? Makayla is a member, and since she stayed with me last night, she couldn't make it here sooner." I glanced at his nametag and manufactured a sweet smile. "Please, Officer Schwartz."

He huffed. "I suppose if I go with you, it'll be okay."

"I'd really appreciate it," Makayla said.

"All right. Let's go." He strolled around the desk.

With Officer Schwartz following, we drove back to the dorm,

where he swiped a card and held the door open for us. We tromped up the stairs. Well, Officer Schwartz and I tromped. Makayla bounced with her pink-streaked ponytail swinging.

"Doesn't this building have an elevator?" I asked as we climbed the second flight.

"Nope," she said. "Try moving a carload of stuff up and down every year."

"Fun times." I'd lived on the first floor of my dorm—a circumstance for which I'd been extremely grateful.

When we arrived at the top, I tried not to pant as we strolled the long, cement-block hall to her room. A whiteboard surrounded by pictures of Makayla and Quincy hung on the door. There wasn't anything remotely creepy about the building, but the lack of students made it feel lifeless.

"I'll wait here." Officer Schwartz took a post across from the door where he had a clear view of the tiny space.

I followed Makayla inside. She and Quincy had lofted their beds and arranged their desks underneath with a mini fridge and bookshelf between. Matching comforters in a purple zig-zag pattern created a fun vibe. The wall opposite the beds contained the closets they'd decorated with photos of friends.

I walked to the window, opened the blinds, and looked out to the center of campus and the chapel. "Nice view."

"Yep." Makayla reached into her closet and took out a black crossbody. On the way over, we'd agreed she'd pretend to have difficulty finding her keys while I snooped—as discreetly as possible.

Makayla's desk held her laptop and was cluttered with framed pictures of her family. The biggest one was of Makayla and her mother. They were both wearing pastel yellow dresses, and I guessed Makayla had about eight. A certificate, declaring Makayla the winner of the Brenneman University Annual Poetry Competition, was tacked to a corkboard above her desk.

With a growl, Makayla shoved the purse back in the closet and grabbed a macramé wristlet. I surveyed Quincy's desk, which was downright sparse compared to Makayla's. A lone family picture rested in the corner of her otherwise bare desk. The corkboard above her desk held a Tune Nutritional Supplements bumper sticker and picture of Quincy and Jonas dressed as Dorothy and the Tin Man. Funny she hadn't removed it.

I scanned the books resting on the shelves—a songwriting textbook, a music theory book, a business principles textbook, and other typical college textbooks for basic classes like world history.

"What'd I do with them?" Makayla threw her hands in the air.

"Try your coat pockets."

"Good idea." She yanked an acid wash denim jacket out of her closet, checked—and then slipped it on.

I peeked in the trashcan next to Quincy's desk, but it was empty. However, a crumpled piece of paper rested next to her chair leg as if she'd missed a shot. I glanced out at the hall. Officer Schwartz had taken out his phone and was gazing at it fondly as his thumbs tapped.

Must be texting a girlfriend since he wasn't wearing a wedding ring.

I bent, swiped the paper, and shoved it into my raincoat pocket. "Hey, Mak. What about your desk?"

This was our code for when I was done snooping.

"I'm so stupid!" she shrieked. "That's exactly what I did with my keys." She stomped over, yanked open the top drawer, and held them up.

"Do you want your laptop?" I asked.

"Yeah." She grabbed the pink shoulder bag and slipped the computer inside.

We turned to go, and Makayla locked the room.

"Did Quincy take her laptop on tour?" I asked as we returned to the hallway.

"Yeah. In her backpack, but I didn't want to drag mine around."

"She left her phone and wallet behind, but she took her laptop? That's weird."

"Definitely." Makayla pocketed her key.

Officer Schwartz looked back and forth between us. "Sure is."

We filed downstairs, and I couldn't leave without trying to extract more information from Officer Schwartz. Maybe he was in a better mood now.

"Have you heard people say why they think Quincy ran off?" I asked.

He held the door open for us. "Not about that, but there's plenty of speculation about her family."

"How so?" I asked.

"I heard through the grapevine they put a ton of pressure on her to live up to their high standards." He closed the door and double-checked to make sure it was locked.

Funny how even a campus policeman knew that. "Most parents want their children to succeed," I said. We stood next to my truck as the sun peeked from behind a cloud.

"But the Ashbrooks are next level." He glanced at Makayla. "At least . . . that's what I've heard."

"Anything specific?" I grabbed my wind-whipped hair to keep it from landing in my lip gloss.

He lowered his voice. "Well, my sister works in housekeeping, and last night my girlfriend and I had dinner with her. We talked about Quincy blowing off the tour and how her dad was raising a stink about the tour going on like nothing happened. Anyways, my sister told me that about a month ago she was cleaning in the music building, and she overheard a professor saying that Quincy Ashbrook's dad had tried to bribe him to get her into Brenneman—even though her grades weren't up to snuff."

"Who was the professor?" I asked.

He waited until a jogger had passed and then cupped his hand next to his mouth. "Dr. Jackson."

# CHAPTER TEN

"Dr. Jackson doesn't work in admissions, so how could he get Quincy in?" Confusion played in Makayla's eyes. The sun disappeared behind a cloud, and she tugged her jacket closed.

"By telling admissions the music department wanted her," I said. "I'm sure she had to audition to be accepted as a music major."

"But she's a fantastic pianist—and has a beautiful voice," Makayla said. "Why would her dad need to bribe Dr. Jackson into telling the truth?"

"Is it hard to get into Brenneman?" I asked.

"Yeah. I had straight A's in high school, and I was wait-listed. I was ready to go to my second choice when I finally got my admissions packet."

"What kind of student is Quincy?"

Makayla chewed her lip. "Not the greatest."

"So it's possible her mom and dad needed to make sure Dr. Jackson recommended Quincy—otherwise she definitely wasn't going to get in."

"Yeah. Even though her dad has donated a ton of money, I doubt the admissions office would've overlooked her poor grades without Dr. Jackson's recommendation." She shifted. "I hope it's not true he took a bribe."

Officer Schwartz tugged his shirt collar. "I'm just telling you what my sister heard, but we don't know Dr. Jackson took the bribe—or even that the Ashbrooks offered him money. You know how stories get twisted." His eyes grew wide. "You're not going to tell anybody, are you? I don't want to lose my job for spreading rumors."

"I'll only mention this to my friend in law enforcement if Quincy doesn't turn up soon."

"All right. I suppose that's fair." He glanced at Makayla. "Enjoy the rest of your break." He moseyed back to his car and drove away.

"What are you thinking?" Makayla asked.

"Officer Schwartz is the second person to mention Quincy being under pressure from her parents, so maybe she *is* chilling at a beach resort."

She sighed. "Then maybe we're just wasting our time."

"Not necessarily. Finding answers is important, and I doubt Quincy ever anticipated her actions would affect so many people."

"Probably not." She finger-combed her ponytail. "Remember her note mentioned there was something she had to take care of. It would be classic Quincy to try to deal with a problem herself. What if somebody found out about her dad bribing Dr. Jackson and was blackmailing her because they know she has money?"

"That's a good theory." As I shoved my hands in my pocket to grab my keys, my fingers brushed against the wadded paper I'd picked up. I uncrumpled it and held the handwritten note out so Makayla could see. "I found this in your room."

Forza 12

"What does *that* mean?" she asked.

I chewed my lip. "*Forza* means force in Italian. Sometimes it's used as a musical term." It was good to know my degree could still come in handy. "I don't know about the twelve. Was Quincy working on an assignment?"

"I'm not sure." Makayla took out her keys and turned toward the parking lot across the street. "She must've been."

---

"Can I feed Gus?" Makayla asked as we entered my back door an hour later.

"Go for it." I disarmed the security system and kicked off my heels, and she took care of my very hyper dog. After the past two days, I was ready for a Sunday afternoon nap before I took on any more investigating. Maybe I'd watch some old episodes of *Murder, She Wrote*. I was halfway across my living room when I froze next to the fireplace and groaned.

I'd volunteered to host my Bible study group tonight.

I surveyed my living room. At least I'd already cleaned off the layer of dust and swept in anticipation of my other guests, which was precisely why I'd volunteered to host two weeks ago. If I was doing all that work, I might as well have two reasons. This still didn't help me with the food problem, and I hadn't even remembered to buy supplies when I'd made a grocery run to get breakfast items for the girls.

I tossed my shoes and purse into my bedroom and returned to the kitchen where Gus was chowing down, and Makayla was at the table scrolling through her phone.

"I forgot I have to host small group tonight," I said.

"Do I need to make myself scarce?" She put her phone on the table.

"Not at all—you're welcome to hang out with us."

"Perfect. I'm ready to think about something besides Quincy. Is Hamlet coming?" Her eyes gleamed.

"Probably." After our talk, I had a feeling he'd be back after skipping our last meeting. I steeled my face, stalked across the kitchen, and opened my refrigerator.

"Cool. I need to determine if he's a better match for you than Cal."

Considering Cal wasn't even an option, I failed to see why that mattered.

"Hamlet's cute," she said. "I'm not a fan of the sweater vest he was wearing today, but he can pull off nerd chic, you know?"

*Life Lesson #429: Ignore annoying things, and they will go away.*

"I need to figure out what to serve." My refrigerator contained creamer, milk, ketchup, pickles—and a package of dubious looking cheddar. I didn't need to search the pantry because I already knew I had canned goods, courtesy of my mom, and cereal.

"Couldn't you order pizza?"

I slammed the refrigerator door and tossed the nasty cheese in the trash. "I've done that the last two times I've hosted."

"What about sandwiches from Velda's?"

"We had that for lunch."

"If I were you, I'd go with pizza. It's super easy and cheap." She tilted her head. "Unless . . . Hamlet doesn't like pizza, and you want to impress him."

So much for annoying things going away.

"We're friends, so if he doesn't already realize I can't cook, he'll know soon. Pizza it is." My friends wouldn't expect anything else, and it was the fellowship that was most important, right? I started emptying my dishwasher.

"I know a great recipe for a chicken casserole that your mom taught me."

"I didn't know she taught you to cook." I stacked plates in my cabinet.

"Yep. I'm her star pupil, and I'd be willing to make the casserole—or teach you to make it since you're putting up with me for a week."

"You'll have to supervise."

"I know. But you'll have to buy the stuff for it. I'm not made of money."

I dealt silverware into the drawer organizer. "Sounds like a plan."

"Now you'll be able to impress Hammie."

I pointed a fork at her. "That's *not* why we're doing this."

"*Sure.* Whatev."

---

"Georgia Rae, this casserole is delicious." Hamlet returned to my dining room with a second helping of King Ranch chicken casserole on his plate. He met my eyes, and there was no mistaking the admiration there.

Makayla smirked.

The rest of my friends—Ashley, my cousin J.T., Dave, Heather, and Evan—were engrossed in a couple of different conversations and didn't appear to notice. Brandi had ditched us to go with her sister to the Parker Curtis concert in Fort Wayne.

"Thanks. Makayla taught me how to make it. If it hadn't been for her, you guys would be eating pizza—again," I said. "My skill set includes calling for food and using the microwave."

He sat in the chair next to mine. "It's refreshing that you aren't perfect."

"Thank you?" How else should I respond to that? Did he know how to cook? Cal's culinary skills were impressive, and if I'd ended up with him—never mind.

"Have there been any new developments in the case with the missing college student?" he asked.

There was a lull in conversation as the rest of my friends looked at me expectantly.

I used my fork to poke a pattern in my empty Styrofoam plate. "It still appears Quincy left on her own, but we don't know why."

Makayla started gathering empty plates. "Quincy has a history of sneaking off, but I'm not convinced that's what happened this time." The distress in her face was obvious.

Evan turned to her. "Do you happen to know my youngest brother—Aidan Beckworth? He's a senior at Brenneman."

*Nice subject change, Evan.* His thoughtfulness had been one of the reasons I'd had a crush on him for three years—until we'd decided we were only meant to be friends.

Makayla's eyes lit up. "Yeah. He's cool. Last year, we had a world history class together, and he was always peeking at my notes. Finally, I had to turn my computer so he could see."

Evan chuckled. "That sounds like him."

"Do Aidan and Quincy know each other?" I looked back and forth between Makayla and Evan.

"Yes—he's the one who told me about Quincy because she's dating his roommate Jonas," Evan said. "He and Aidan have a house off campus with a few other guys."

So often Evan provided valuable information and didn't even realize it. "What's your brother doing this week?"

He pushed his empty plate away. "He's been hanging out at a friend's house this weekend, but he's coming over tomorrow.

We're going to play tennis at the indoor courts and hit the driving range." Evan, a guidance counselor at the local high school, was also on spring break.

"Is there any chance Aidan might be able to talk to me?" I asked.

Makayla cleared her throat—loudly.

"I mean, talk to Makayla and me. I'd like to see what he knows about Quincy and Jonas."

"He probably wouldn't mind." Evan took a drink. "How about joining us for doubles?"

"Yes! I love tennis." Makayla pumped her fist. "It's like the one sport I'm decent at. Dad made me take lessons when I was a kid."

I hadn't played tennis since high school PE class. "I'm not sure—"

"It'll be fun." Evan tossed his napkin on his plate. "We'll play mixed doubles. You and me against Makayla and Aidan."

"I like that," she said. "The young versus the old."

I stifled a groan. "Yay."

---

Monday morning, drizzle cast a gloomy pall over my home, and I would've preferred to stay in, drinking coffee and tweaking our crop plan for the upcoming planting season. Instead, I'd agreed to tennis torture.

As Makayla and I were heading out to meet Evan and his brother, I opened my garage door and discovered Detective Vanessa Hawk emerging from her car. The willowy, auburn-haired detective looked more like she should be modeling instead of interrogating suspects. Last month, when she'd started working with Cal, I'd been relieved to discover she was engaged.

Speaking of Cal, why wasn't he with Vanessa?

"Morning, ladies." She entered my garage and surveyed us without a hint of the friendliness I'd experienced on the double date with Cal, Vanessa, and her fiancé Curtis. Beads of moisture clung to her black trench coat.

"What's going on?" I shoved my hands in my jacket pockets.

"I need to ask the two of you a few questions about Elias Kurtz." Her expression grew severe.

*Uh-oh.*

"What about him?" Makayla asked as the tennis bag she'd retrieved from her trunk slid from her shoulder.

"He was found dead in his car at Briarwick Cemetery, and the two of you were among the last people to see him alive."

## CHAPTER ELEVEN

"That's awful!" I wrapped my arms around my waist and shivered.

Makayla's tennis bag plopped onto the concrete. Her hand flew to her mouth, and tears welled in her eyes. "Wh-when was he found?"

"Yesterday morning." Vanessa narrowed her eyes and rested her gaze on Makayla and then me. "The cemetery's maintenance man reported finding Elias's body in an abandoned car."

"How'd he die?" I asked.

"Shot in the chest."

Makayla winced.

Vanessa furrowed her brow. "I'm surprised you didn't hear about his murder on the news last night."

"We were very busy yesterday," I said. "Is Quincy Ashbrook involved in his death?"

Makayla's eyes widened.

"You know I can't discuss an active investigation." Vanessa studied us, and it was clear she was reading *us* for any signs of guilt.

"How can we help?" I rested my hand on my stepsister's arm and faced Vanessa. "And where's Cal, by the way?"

Her eyes flashed. "We'll get to Detective Perkins in a minute. Tell me what you were doing in Elias Kurtz's dressing room on Saturday night. I have a witness who saw you both go in."

Makayla hunched over and shoved her hands in her raincoat pockets.

*Maria.* She must've remembered our names from the meet and greet. Elias had called Makayla by name, and she'd introduced me.

"Well?" Vanessa tapped her foot.

Makayla clearly wasn't going to speak, so I'd better nip this problem in the bud. "After Quincy disappeared, one of my sources—"

"Be specific," Vanessa said. "Tell me who you talked to."

Vanessa's girl-next-door looks had to be her superpower. They were disarming and friendly, and then out of nowhere, bad cop showed up.

*Cal, where are you?*

"Bobbi Sue Miller at Latte Conspiracies," I said.

"Go on." Vanessa withdrew a small notebook and pen from her jacket pocket and scribbled on the paper—very old school.

"Bobbi Sue said a handsome man in a Brenneman University jacket came in and asked about Quincy. He had a picture of them together. Based on Bobbi Sue's description, Makayla guessed it was Dr. Kurtz. When she showed Bobbi Sue his picture, she confirmed it."

"He doesn't work at Brenneman anymore." Makayla hovered at my elbow.

"I'm aware. So the two of you thought you'd play detectives and talk to Elias about Quincy after the show." Vanessa arched one eyebrow.

"Pretty much." There was no point in denying it. "I paid

good money for the meet and greet. Besides, I was going to call Cal today and let him know that Quincy was part of Elias's downline in the Tune Nutritional Supplement Company. I suspect he may've had a romantic relationship with her—though he denied it."

Makayla studied her tennis shoes.

Vanessa scrawled on her notepad. "You should report anything pertaining to this case to me. Detective Perkins is taking time off."

My eyes widened. "Why? Is he okay? Is it because he's moving?"

"If he wanted you to know, he would've told you." She lifted her chin.

Her words gut-punched me, but I admired her loyalty. Though I wasn't thrilled to be pegged as the evil ex-girlfriend. That was a role I'd never played before, since Cal had been my first actual boyfriend. "Is it because his mom is visiting?"

She consulted her notepad. "Did you learn anything else from Elias?"

I smothered a sigh. "Dr. Jackson was the one who told Elias Quincy had run off."

"Speaking of Dr. Jackson . . ." Vanessa surveyed Makayla. "When I met with him, he mentioned you asked to leave the tour prior to it being cancelled. Why?"

"I wanted to figure out what happened with Quincy." She ducked her head.

Vanessa scribbled. "Do you believe your roommate is in danger?"

"My gut says *yes*, but I've been going back and forth in my head for two days and can't come up with a specific threat."

Vanessa scrawled more notes. "Did you take classes from Elias Kurtz at Brenneman?"

"He was my voice teacher freshman year."

"Did your relationship with him extend beyond the classroom?"

Makayla blushed. "No. I had a crush on him, but he was always professional with me."

If we were suspects in this case—and I wasn't convinced we were—then we needed to wrap up this conversation and talk to a lawyer. "Vanessa—"

"It'd be best if you called me Detective Hawk." She gave me a tolerant half smile that reminded me of her predecessor, Detective Marvin Kimball.

Did trainers teach that expression at the police academy? I pictured a room full of recruits practicing stern facial expressions and had to battle a snicker.

"My apologies, Detective Hawk," I said. "If you don't have any more questions, then Makayla and I need to be on our way. We're meeting some friends to play tennis."

"One more question—for both of you. Where were you Sunday between one and three in the morning?"

"We were here. Sleeping," I said.

Makayla's face had lost all trace of color.

"Was there anyone else here?"

I looked her in the eyes. "No, ma'am."

"I'll be in touch." Detective Hawk slipped her notebook in her jacket pocket and turned toward her car.

"Detective Hawk?" I said.

"Yes." She faced me.

"I didn't want to break up with Cal. I needed him to be more open with me about his life, but he refused."

"I see." She flipped her hair over her shoulder.

"I really cared about him. I still do."

"He cared about you." She took a menacing step toward me. "You could've been a little more patient with someone going through what he's dealing with."

"I tried to be as understanding as I could about his parents' divorce—"

"I'm not talking about their divorce," she snapped. "That's old news."

The day we'd broken up, he'd alluded to something going on, but when I'd asked, he'd told me his life wasn't a mystery I needed to solve. "Then what do—?"

"Never mind." She wrenched open her car door. "Forget I said anything."

Makayla and I stood frozen as Detective Hawk zoomed out of my driveway.

"I can't believe Dr. Kurtz is dead—and that she thinks we killed him," Makayla whispered.

I curled my fingers around my keys. "I don't think she does, but she has to rule us out." For Makayla's sake, I was trying really hard to stay calm.

"Are you sure?"

"No. But now it's even more critical that we figure out what's going on, so we'll play tennis as planned. Aidan might know something important."

She swallowed. "Okay."

We got in my truck, and I handed Makayla my phone. "Text Evan and tell him we're running a few minutes late."

---

Back in high school, my best friend Laura had wanted to catch the attention of Richardville High School's number one tennis player. Journey O'Neill was a handsome stud on his way to earning a college scholarship at an NCAA Division One school. Laura was a decent player herself and earned the number two spot on the Wildcat Springs team. They'd met at a tournament the previous summer and had been talking ever since.

One fall afternoon, she needed a wingwoman and dragged me into Richardville to watch Journey play his sectional match. We shouldn't have bothered. Journey won 6-0, 6-0, but not before his hopelessly mismatched opponent lobbed one of Journey's power shots over the fence where it rocketed to the bleachers and slammed smack dab into my cheekbone.

The ball left an ugly bruise that took a couple of weeks to fade and caused rumors about me being knocked around by a boy —never mind that I wasn't dating anyone—and Laura had decided that arrogant Journey wasn't for her.

This fear of tennis balls loomed in my mind when Makayla handed me her extra racket as we walked from the locker rooms to the courts inside the Richard County Tennis Center. Since I didn't have a cute red and white striped vintage dress like my stepsister, I'd settled for a faded Wildcat Springs High School T-shirt and black athletic shorts that displayed my pasty legs.

Evan waved us over to where he waited next to the net with his handsome, look-alike little brother. I introduced myself to Aidan, who had sandy hair and hazel eyes. While Evan's eyes were kind, Aidan's held a spark of mischief.

"Sorry we're late. Detective Hawk paid us a visit this morning," I said.

Evan cracked open a new can of tennis balls, and a rubbery scent hissed out. "What'd you do now?" He tossed a ball to his brother.

I gave him a quick recap while Aidan stared at me.

"I can't believe Dr. Kurtz is gone. He was such a great guy." Makayla shuddered. "Who'd want to kill him?"

"Obviously someone you don't want to mess with." Evan leveled his gaze at me. "Sounds like a good reason for you to back off your investigating."

"Or all the more reason to find Quincy." Like a lot of my friends, Evan didn't understand my need to find justice—or answers for the victims' families. But they hadn't lost a parent to murder and lived without answers for nearly a decade.

Evan picked up his racket. "Just be careful."

"We will." I tugged my T-shirt hem.

Aidan tossed a tennis ball in the air and caught it. "I don't mean to sound insensitive, but the clock's ticking. We've only got the court for two hours."

"Right. Let's do this." Makayla took her racket out of her bag.

Aidan turned to Makayla. "I hear it's us against the old people."

She gave him a high five. "That's right. You two are going down." They sauntered around the net.

*Yep. I know.*

"Evan, I'm sorry, but I haven't played since high school," I whispered.

"I didn't know you were on the team." He coached the high school boys.

"I wasn't. I meant sophomore PE class." I said a silent prayer of thanks that the other courts were empty.

*Just three witnesses.*

"No worries." He smiled. "I'll give you pointers and serve first."

"Good call. I'll just stand by the net and do what I can." At least I was tall. I bent at the waist and spun the racket in my hands, trying to look like Laura had when I'd watched her matches.

"Love all." Evan tossed the ball in the air, and before I knew what was happening, Aidan returned the serve. The ball whizzed by my shoulder, and Evan caught it with his backhand.

Makayla returned the shot, and the menacing yellow bullet barreled toward me. I raised my racket up in self-defense, and the ball doinked off of it and dropped on our side of the court.

*Help me, Jesus.*

I snatched up the evil projectile and tossed it to Evan.

"Nice try, Georgia." Evan moved to the left side of the court.

I scooted right but kept my post near the net.

"Love fifteen."

This time I was prepared for the speed of the game—or so I thought. After a nice volley between Aidan and Evan, Makayla smashed the ball toward me.

I swung—and missed. The ball grazed my arm and plunked inside the lines before rolling away.

Makayla and Aidan cheered.

I trotted to the court next to ours, retrieved the ball, and tossed it to Evan. "Sorry."

"No worries. Love thirty."

This time Evan got smart, and after volleying with his brother, he charged the net and put away the return shot with a wicked backspin.

"Nice!" I hadn't moved. How long would this match take? Hadn't Laura talked about something called an eight-game pro set? I should suggest one so Evan and Aidan could enjoy their time on the court.

"Thanks." Evan sauntered back to serve. "Fifteen thirty."

By this time, I'd figured out my role—and Life Lesson #6753: *Stay out of the way, and let your teammate handle the game. Swing only in self-defense.*

Actually, I was pretty certain I could also apply that advice to criminal investigations—but that wasn't going to happen.

---

Everyone liked my suggestion of an eight-game pro set, and after Aidan and Makayla beat Evan and me eight to five, we let the boys finish their time on the court while we waited in the elevated lobby, watching through the floor-to-ceiling window.

I collapsed on the brown leather sectional sofa facing the courts. "I'm beat."

"You barely moved." Makayla smoothed her hair.

"I'm exhausted from the stress." I propped my feet up on the coffee table full of tennis magazines. I'd already changed into long pants—no one else needed to see me in those shorts.

She laughed. "Anyway, Aidan's pretty cool—and cute. It's nice to see him outside of class."

Maybe my embarrassment over my lack of tennis prowess was worth it if there was a love connection. "Does he have a girlfriend?"

"I don't know. But I'll find out." She removed her phone, and I guessed she was stalking him on social media.

A few minutes later, she wiggled her phone in triumph. "If he does, it's on the down-low. No pics of a girl. Just guys on the tennis team and his roommates."

"Good deal." While she continued her online research, I took out my phone and found an article about Elias Kurtz's death. The *Richard County Gazette* had an article on their website.

Actor found dead at local cemetery

RICHARDVILLE — The Richard County Sheriff's Department reports that a maintenance worker at Briarwick Cemetery in rural Richard County discovered a body in an abandoned car early Sunday morning. The victim was thirty-two-year-old actor Elias Kurtz, who was currently starring in *The Sound of Music* at Bell's Dinner Theater in Richardville. Kurtz's death has been ruled a homicide.

Anyone with information pertaining to this case is encouraged to contact the sheriff's department.

I dropped my phone in my lap. It was very strange that Elias had died at a cemetery and Quincy had disappeared at one. Still, the article didn't reveal anything new or helpful.

I watched Evan and Aidan volley and considered everything we'd learned, and there was one area where I hadn't followed up.

"Mak, what can you tell me about Dr. Jackson?"

"Not much. He's a bachelor. His house is a few blocks from campus, and he walks to work when the weather's nice. He expects a lot out of his students, so he's all business when it comes to music."

"Is he the type to take a bribe?"

"I've been thinking about that since we talked to Officer Schwartz." She slouched and crossed her arms. "Under the right circumstances, anybody might be tempted to take a bribe, so I have no idea. I'm sorry."

"No worries. I don't expect you to be a mind reader." I used my phone to locate the music department's page on the university website, found the faculty biographies, and opened Dr. Jackson's. His picture showed a thinner—almost gaunt—man.

"Check this out." I turned my phone toward Makayla. "Was he sick?"

"Yeah. I'd forgotten he had cancer. We had a fundraiser for him the fall of my freshman year."

"When was he diagnosed?"

"Earlier that year, I think." She turned her attention back to her own phone. Apparently, Aidan's life was riveting.

"What if . . ." I waited for her to look up. "Medical bills would've been great motivation for accepting a bribe from Quincy's dad."

"Yeah." She winced. "You're right."

A while later, Evan and Aidan finished their match and came into the lobby.

"He beat me." Aidan adjusted the tennis bag on his shoulder.

Evan pointed his thumbs at his chest. "This old man's still got it."

"Oh, shut up." Aidan punched Evan's arm. "Thirty-two isn't old."

I looked at Evan. "Two hours ago, you were old."

"What can I say?" Evan grinned and held up his phone. "Excuse me a minute. Kelsey called, so I'm going to see if I can catch her." He walked over to the corner next to a drinking fountain. His girlfriend worked at a clinic in Ethiopia, and the distance was hard on them both.

"Aidan, Makayla and I are trying to figure out what's going on with Quincy Ashbrook. Do you mind if I ask a few questions about your roommate?"

"Jo-Bro? Sure." He dropped his bag and took a drink from his thermos. "Fire away."

"Did you know he and Quincy split a couple of weeks ago?" I asked.

"For real? He was hanging out with her last weekend." He set his thermos next to his bag and plopped onto the sofa next to Makayla.

"Yes. Jonas told us they were still friends. Did Quincy spend a lot of time at your house?"

"Some." He took a tennis ball from his pocket and bounced it. "She's cool."

"Tell me about Jonas."

"Jo-Bro's pretty quiet. That's why he's an awesome roommate. Half the time you don't even know he's around, and he doesn't leave his stuff everywhere. Plus, he's cool to hang out with."

Great. We'd established Jo-Bro and Quincy were cool. *Riveting information . . . Nice Georgia.* "What else can you tell me about him?"

"He's from Indy. Business major. Marketing minor. Loves working out and is a health nut. Plays lead guitar in a band." He bounced the ball some more. "The dude loves pranks. He's pulled off some epic stunts."

"What's his best one?" I asked.

Aidan pocketed the tennis ball. "Freshman year, we had a scavenger hunt pick-a-date, and Jo helped plan it. Anyway, one of the tasks was to stop at a cemetery and get a picture of a grave- stone of someone named John."

Jonas had sent people to a cemetery. Interesting. Makayla crossed her arms.

"So my buddies, our dates, and I are strolling through the cemetery, when Jo pops out from behind a headstone. The dude's dressed like a zombie and starts chasing us."

Quite the stunt for a guy with coimetrophobia. "I bet that was startling."

"Sure was. But we cracked up after we stopped screaming."

What else had Jonas lied about? What if instead of being afraid, he was obsessed with cemeteries and had arranged the meetings with Quincy and Elias? If he were trying to creep them out, it could be a very effective—and private—meeting place.

"This may sound weird, but did you ever see Quincy with two phones?"

"No." Aidan dabbed a towel over his face and furrowed his brow. "But speaking of second phones, something weird happened last week." He tossed the towel over his shoulder. "Some of the guys in my house and I were watching *Dumb and Dumber* when our couch vibrated. I found a phone between the cushions. Jo claimed it was his buddy's, but then he acted all guilty and stuck it in his pocket like it was his and he didn't want us to see. I don't know. Maybe it really was his friend's. Jo's phone was sitting out on the coffee table, so he wasn't hiding *that*."

"Did he mention his buddy's name?" I asked.

"Nope."

That would've been too easy. "Was it a burner phone?"

He leaned back into the sofa. "Could've been. It was a smartphone, but it looked pretty cheap."

"Did you happen to see who the call was from?" I asked.

"Janebug—no last name."

Makayla sat up straighter.

I stared at her.

"Janebug is Jonas's nickname for Quincy."

## CHAPTER TWELVE

"Jo never told me that." Aidan shrugged. "But we don't tell each other everything."

"Probably because he didn't want you to know she called him Jobug." Makayla snickered. "Jane's her middle name, but I don't know where they got *bug*." She made a gagging motion.

"Did Jonas ever seem to be hiding anything besides the phone?" I asked.

"I don't think so, but he could've been." Aidan furrowed his brow. "We've already established I had no idea what he called his girlfriend."

I smothered a grin. "Did he run errands at odd hours? Stay out late often?"

"Sometimes. Last year when we lived in the dorm, we didn't have a curfew, so he took advantage of that." He put the towel around his neck and held onto both ends. "Now the guys and I share a house—well, it's a remodeled church—and we all have our own rooms. If Jonas is coming and going late at night, I wouldn't hear him. I'm a really heavy sleeper."

"That's true." Evan pocketed his phone as he rejoined us. "He had to be since he was the baby of the family."

"How's Kelsey?" She and I were prayer partners and emailed on a fairly regular basis.

"We didn't have long to talk, but she wanted to tell me she's coming home this summer for a visit."

For a second, I thought he was going to jump up and down. "That's great. How long will she be here?" We all got up and headed for the parking lot.

"A month." He beamed.

Outside the door, Aidan froze next to a bench. "Wait. I just remembered something else that might be important."

We stopped. At least the drizzle had ended, and the sun had made an appearance.

"What's that?" I asked.

"About a month ago, I came home to study between classes. Jo's room is right next to mine, and I heard his phone ring. Then he yelled, 'He can't quit! What're we going to do?' It was weird because I'd never heard Jo freak out like that before."

In spite of the warmer temperature, goosebumps rose on my arms. "Anything else?"

"Just a thump—like he pounded his fist against the wall."

---

"Now what?" Makayla asked as we heated leftover chicken casserole for lunch.

The microwave dinged, and I grabbed hot pads and removed the ceramic dish. "Get the plates. We're eating in the dining room."

"Why?" But she—and Gus—followed me.

I set the casserole on the table and pointed at the chalkboard I'd painted on my dining room wall and trimmed with reclaimed wood. Last night, Ashley had drawn a picture of a kitten pawing a ball of yarn, and I hoped she wasn't leaving visual hints for me to get an indoor cat the way she'd campaigned for me to get a dog.

Gus would *not* appreciate a feline roommate.

"We're going to write what we already know about the case on the board," I said.

"That's awesome!" She sat and started eating.

I took a bite and grabbed a piece of blue chalk from the basket on the sideboard. "Let's make a timeline." I scooped up a bite of casserole and chewed while I drew a line and notches. "Quincy left Saturday morning sometime after midnight. Cal found my abandoned car between six-thirty and seven. We know from Detective Hawk asking for our whereabouts that Elias must've been murdered between one and three on Sunday morning." I added these events and turned to Makayla. "What am I missing?"

She studied the board. "The chorale got back to Brenneman late Saturday night." She scrolled through her phone. "Sammi's text came in at 11:46."

I added that, took another bite, and considered everything that'd happened. I wrote *Quincy, Jonas, Elias,* and *Dr. Jackson* on the board, along with *Tune Nutritional Supplements, burner phone, no ransom, bad blood between Elias and Dr. Jackson,* and *Jonas angry about something and lying about fear of cemeteries.* "I hate to bring this up, but—"

"You've been wondering if Quincy could've shot Dr. Kurtz."

"Yes."

"She wouldn't do that." Makayla's expression dared me to challenge her.

"How can you be sure? Detective Hawk didn't deny the possibility of Quincy's involvement."

"I just know."

Not this again. I closed my eyes. *Lord, give me patience.* I flicked the chalk between my fingers and considered Makayla's reactions. "I know you're worried about being a good example for Quincy, but why else are you so loyal to her?"

Makayla pushed a glob of casserole around her plate and dropped her fork. "Freshman year, I struggled with depression."

"I remember."

"The transition to college was hard for me, and I had trouble making friends first semester—except for Quincy. I wasn't easy to live with, and for some reason she stuck by me, so I owe it to her to figure out if she's in danger." Makayla twisted her napkin. "Is she spoiled? Yes. Selfish? Definitely. A murderer? No way."

Makayla's certainty did nothing to alleviate my doubts, but I needed to keep her on my side if we were going to get to the bottom of the situation. "Okay. We'll look at a different angle." I squinted at the board. "Dr. Jackson had time to make it to Richardville after the chorale returned. What if Elias discovered Dr. Jackson took a bribe from Quincy's parents and threatened to expose him? Elias could've been trying to get revenge for not getting his contract renewed."

"I have trouble picturing Dr. Jackson shooting anyone," she said. "He has high standards, but he seems so harmless."

I was probably getting cynical, but I'd learned that even the most harmless looking people were capable of murder.

Makayla leaned back. "Quincy's parents would've been affected if Dr. Kurtz exposed the bribery, and her dad is super intense."

"Enough to kill Elias?"

She squeezed her napkin. "I always thought Mr. Ashbrook was a nice guy—at least until he had a cow when he was here . . . so . . . maybe?"

I studied the timeline. "Jonas had time to make it to Richardville as well. What if he was more upset by the breakup than we realized, and he was jealous of Quincy's relationship with Elias?"

Makayla compressed her lips. "Dr. Kurtz said he wasn't seeing Quincy."

I took a bite of casserole to keep myself from arguing. "The chick who played Maria in *The Sound of Music* was giving us the evil eye when she saw us going into Elias's dressing room, so maybe she had a thing for him. We should talk to her."

"She probably reported us to Detective Hawk, so I doubt she'll talk to us."

"We should try," I said. "She had on a Fitness Universe Staff sweatshirt, so we could find her there. Do you remember seeing her name in the program?"

"Kimberlee Samson. She spells *Kimberlee* with a double *ee* on the end."

"I'd love to go now." I dropped the chalk in the basket. "But I need to inspect my planter this afternoon." After all, I had to be ready to get in the field when the weather turned.

"I'll call Fitness Universe and see if I can figure out Kimberlee's work schedule," Makayla said. "If she's around when you're done, we can go see her. I have an essay that's due a few days after break, so I should be a responsible adult too."

"Sounds good."

After we finished eating, Makayla went upstairs, and I headed outside to my pole barn where Grandpa and I stored equipment. When I slid the large metal doors aside and flicked on the lights, my gray striped cat sprang off the workbench in the corner. He rubbed around my legs as I patted his head. Since the afternoon was pleasant, I left the doors open to get some air circulating.

Seeing the planter caused a surge of excitement for the upcoming season. I turned on some choral music, and a while later, I was in the middle of examining seed tubes for wear when Makayla ran in.

"Georgia!"

My orange cat skittered into a corner next to a tractor and eyed my stepsister from behind a tire.

I walked around the planter. "What?"

She waved a scrap of paper. "I found a note in Quincy's chorale dress pocket."

# CHAPTER THIRTEEN

M y mind raced. "What does it say?"
She held the note so I could see.

You can't ignore this deadline. Meet BB at Fillmore Cemetery.
1:00 a.m. Saturday.

Someone had printed the note in blue ink, and the paper had been torn from one of the attendance pads at my church, because the church's logo remained on the back side. "Whoever slipped Quincy the note was at the concert." I studied the rumpled paper. "What deadline?"

"I wish I knew. Whatever it was, it sounds like she was mixed up in something bad." Makayla wrapped her arms around her waist and bounced up and down on her toes.

"Any idea who BB is?"

"No. I can't even think of someone with those initials."

I couldn't either. We walked out of the barn, and I slid the doors shut. "What made you think to look in Quincy's dress pocket?"

"I was trying to write my essay but got stuck. I thought about everything that's happened to see if I could remember anything strange." She followed me across the driveway, the gravel crunching under our feet. "Sammi and I couldn't find Quincy at the church after the concert."

"Yeah." I held the back door open. "I thought she went to the restroom."

Makayla hovered at the door. "That's what she said, but right after the concert was over, we all went before you met us in the chapel. I didn't think about her going again because I figured she didn't feel well. But when she came around the corner, she had a piece of paper in her hand."

I didn't recall seeing it, but I remembered her sulky posture. "Right before she shoved her hands in her pockets?" I crossed the kitchen, grabbed a baggie from the pantry, and handed it to Makayla.

"Yep." She slid the note inside. "What should we do now?"

I closed the pantry door. "We're going to see Detective Hawk. She needs to look at this note."

Tears pooled in Makayla's eyes. "I'm really scared for Quincy."

I rested my hand on her shoulder. "I know. We'll do what we can to help and keep praying."

---

Makayla and I entered the Richard County Sheriff's Department, and the twenty-something receptionist, whom I'd always figured had a crush on Cal, greeted us.

"We need to see Detective Hawk as soon as she's available."

There was no mistaking the smug look on the receptionist's face as she flipped her bangs out of her eyes and picked up the phone. "I'll let her know you're here, Georgia. Have a seat."

We perched on the hard, plastic chairs, and Makayla tapped her foot against the worn tile.

"Do you remember seeing Quincy talking to anyone after the concert?" I asked.

She closed her eyes. "I can't remember. It wasn't that long between when we went to the restroom and you met us in the chapel."

A door opened, and the dark-haired woman that I'd seen on Saturday in Latte Conspiracies exited, followed by Detective Hawk. The woman wore a leopard-print trench coat and skinny jeans with a frayed hem.

"I trust you won't mention what we've discussed to my son." The woman's stern expression left no room for argument.

Then I recognized her voice.

*Cal's mom.* I hadn't identified her from the few pictures I'd seen in Cal's apartment because, after her divorce, she'd let her short hair grow past her shoulders and had cosmetic work done.

*Botox? Facelift? Nose job?* I couldn't decide.

"You have my word. I'll be in touch if I find out anything new." Detective Hawk gripped the edge of the door.

"Thank you." Yvonne turned, and our eyes met. "Georgia Rae Winston!" She croaked. "I shouldn't be surprised—running into you here. Come over here, dear. Let me give you a hug." She didn't wait for me to cross the room, and instead, closed the gap and threw her arms—and the aroma of cigarettes and vanilla—around me. "Don't you give up on that son of mine," she whispered as she gripped my upper arms. "He'll come around one of these days. Yvonne doesn't like that baker chick he went out with. Too perky." She released her vise grip on my appendages and barged out the door as if she were ready to grab the world by its shirt collar.

Detective Hawk blew out a breath. "Come on back, ladies."

She led us through a maze of desks and stopped next to a pair of desks that faced each other.

Cal's workspace was clear except for his computer.

"Have a seat." She motioned to two chairs she'd arranged beside her desk, which was strewn with papers and held a picture of her with her fiancé. They were planning to marry in April.

We sat, and Makayla thrust the baggie toward the detective. "I found this note in Quincy's dress pocket."

Detective Hawk took the bag. "Thank you. How did—?" Her phone rang. "Hawk." She listened. "Okay." She disconnected and stood. "I need to take care of something for another case. I'll be back in a minute." She left Quincy's note on her desk and hurried away.

My eyes fell on a pale green sticky note attached to her computer monitor. *Yvonne Conner* was scribbled on the paper—followed by a phone number. Underneath, was the name *Mason Thrailkill.*

Cal's best friend from Ohio—who was also a detective.

Yvonne had worked as a homicide detective in Cleveland, and while it made sense for her to visit and help Cal move, why was she talking to Detective Hawk without Cal knowing? Was Mason involved in whatever situation Yvonne had been discussing with Detective Hawk? Was that what Cal had refused to tell me about? If so, why?

"Are you okay?" Makayla tapped my arm. "You zoned out."

"Yeah." I blinked. "I'm trying to figure out what Cal's mom was doing."

"I wouldn't get in her way if I were you."

"That's solid advice."

"Which you're going to ignore."

"Maybe." *Probably.*

Detective Hawk returned from a back hallway. "Sorry about

that." She rolled out her desk chair and sat. "Do know who BB is?"

"No."

"Did you see who gave Quincy the note?" Detective Hawk asked.

"No." Makayla folded and unfolded her hands. "I'm sorry."

"Are we suspects in Elias Kurtz's murder?" I asked.

"No. Other than the two of you talking to Elias on Saturday night, there's no evidence that suggests you're involved."

"Do you have a suspect?"

"We've been through this." Detective Hawk glared at me. "You know I can't say."

"You know I can't help trying." I hoped she wouldn't change her name when she got married because her fierce expression was so . . . hawk-like. I fought a badly timed giggle.

As if she could read my thoughts, Detective Hawk narrowed her eyes and rose. "Thanks for turning in the note. I'll be in touch if I have any more questions." She collected Makayla's phone number and walked us toward the exit.

"One more thing." I paused next to the door that led to the waiting area.

"I'm not going to tell you why Cal's mom was here." Detective Hawk folded her arms, but her eyes glimmered with amusement.

Makayla emitted a fake-sounding cough punctuated with a giggle.

"Does her visit have something to do with Mason Thrailkill?"

Detective Hawk patted my arm. "You've got some nice investigative chops. Figure it out." She held my gaze and opened the door.

I took that as a solid *yes*.

We left the building, and as soon as we were in my truck, Makayla leaned back against the headrest. "Now what?"

My mind was whirling in five directions, but I needed to pick one and go with it. "Did you call Fitness Universe and get Kimberlee's work schedule?"

"I got so caught up in the note that I completely forgot."

"No problem. Since we're already in town, let's just drop in and see if she's working."

---

When Makayla and I arrived at Fitness Universe, we marched straight to the front desk. This wasn't the first time I'd been to this gym in a quest for information, but the scrawny kid working was unfamiliar. With his slouchy back to the desk, he wore earbuds and bobbed his head to a steady beat. A Tune Nutritional Supplements water bottle rested next to a desktop computer.

I stood at the counter and stared at him.

A few seconds later, he whipped around with wide eyes and yanked out the earbuds. "Sorry. What can I do for you?" His nametag read *Otis*.

I motioned to Makayla. "We'd like information on purchasing memberships."

"Sure." He grabbed a couple of brochures and slid them across the counter. "We have several plans." When his eyes fell on Makayla, his slumped posture went on hiatus. "We offer a two-week trial, so we can show you what we've got."

*This is all you, Makayla.*

"Cool. My friend Kimberlee Samson raves about this place. Do you know her?" She flipped her hair over her shoulder and leaned against the counter.

"Yeah. She teaches cycling classes." Otis moved closer to Makayla and lowered his voice. "She's a real drill sergeant, so don't take her sessions unless you want a *serious* workout."

Makayla waved a hand. "I *love* a good workout, so I'm sold. How do we sign up for the trial?"

Sign up? She couldn't have just pretended?

"I just need to see some ID, and I'll get you going."

*Oh, goodie.*

We produced our driver's licenses, and after taking our information, Otis handed us two temporary cards. "These are good for the next two weeks, and you can take advantage of any of our classes. After the trial period expires, you'll need to select one of our membership packages if you're still interested."

"Do you have a class schedule?" she asked.

"You can find them on our app or our website. Put in the zip code for this location, and you'll have a complete schedule."

"Cool." Makayla smiled at him.

"Thanks, Otis. By the way." I pointed to his water bottle. "How do you like your Tune Supplements?"

"They're awesomesauce. Tempo is my favorite because it gives me tons of energy when I drink it in the morning. Chord is a solid multivitamin." He lowered his voice. "I'm going to have to find a new sales rep, though. Mine was the guy who got shot at Briarwick Cemetery on Saturday night. Did you hear about that?"

What a small world. "Yeah. Pretty scary and sad."

"Did he workout here?" Makayla asked.

"All the time." Otis shook his head. "Elias was a great dude. He and your friend Kimberlee had just started dating—but you probably already knew that."

*No, no we didn't.* "It's certainly a tragic situation." I held up my pass. "Thanks again for your help."

"Enjoy your trial." He fixed his gaze on Makayla before putting his earbuds back in place and resuming the head bobbing.

We huddled near the door as Makayla downloaded the app. "Got the schedule." She tapped a few times. "Most of her classes are in the mornings, but Kimberlee's teaching a beginning cycling class today at five."

Since Bell's Dinner Theater was closed on Mondays, that made sense.

"We have time to go to your house, change, and get back here, right?" she asked.

I glanced at my watch. 4:03. "I suppose."

"Let's go." She charged out the door.

I set my jaw and followed. How bad could one cycling class be?

---

Precisely one hour and twenty-seven minutes after Makayla and I had made the decision to take a cycling class, I knew what eternal torment felt like.

My ample thighs burned with a searing fire I didn't know was possible. Kimberlee rode her bike and barked out commands as her ponytail swished back and forth. My backside protested from being squished against the seat. With all the inventions created during the last century, someone couldn't have designed a more comfortable bike seat?

And did I mention, Taryn Anderson was on the bike in front of me looking as perky as she had on her date with my ex-boyfriend? How was it even possible to look so cute while enduring torture?

In that moment, I was completely convinced there was no luck quite like Georgia Rae Winston Luck.

Next to me, Makayla was winded but keeping up with Kimberlee's orders.

I pressed a towel against my forehead but didn't stop moving my legs for fear Kimberlee would call me out. She'd already done that to a couple of teenage guys she thought were slacking.

Would I even be able to limp tomorrow?

Ten minutes later, Kimberlee told us to take a break. I slid off the bike and wobbled on gelatin legs. I latched onto the bike for support.

"Are you okay?" Makayla whispered.

"I've been better," I wheezed and took a drink.

"I'm going to refill my water." She grabbed her bottle and left the room.

Taryn turned around, her top knot wobbling. "Oh, my goodness, Georgia! How's it going? I haven't seen you in my shop for a while." She looked me up and down. "Wait. Don't tell me. You're on a diet. That's why." She stuck out her lip. "Don't forget my bakery if you have a cheat day."

"Cheating isn't my thing," I said.

"I can tell. You've lost what, ten pounds?"

Maybe I liked her after all and could forgive her for dating my ex-boyfriend. "You're so sweet to say that!" I'd probably gained ten pounds since the breakup. I didn't have a scale, but my jeans were snug because I'd been hitting the chocolate chip cookie dough ice cream a little too hard. "Have you been working out here for long?"

"Since January. This is the first year I've kept my New Year's resolutions longer than a week."

"Good for you." How could I segue to Cal?

Taryn might spill more information than Detective Hawk had surrendered. Was there a graceful—or casual—way to achieve that without seeming like a nosy ex-girlfriend?

It wouldn't hurt to try. "It's always good to be healthy. Not to mention the men in your life might appreciate the results."

"Yeah. I suppose." Her eyes gleamed. "How are things going with Hamlet?"

"Hamlet and I are friends." I kept my tone light, even though I wanted to punch Miss Smirky Pants in the throat.

"Not for long, if he gets his way. If there's one thing I know about Hamlet Miller, it's that he's persistent. We dated in high school, you know." She gazed at me as if she couldn't wait to see how I reacted.

I was pretty sure my brother had told me Hamlet and Taryn had just been friends, but I commanded my face to produce a smile. *She's not getting a rise out of me. No way, no how.* "I remember seeing you guys in my brother's prom pictures." In that moment I was certain if I weren't a farmer, I'd take the first job I could find far away from Central Indiana where there were plenty of available guys who didn't know me—or anyone from my past. "How are things going with Cal?" My voice was a little too squeaky to pass for cool.

*Life Lesson #384: Never let yourself be outdone.*

"They're great. He's amazing. Guys like him don't come along every day."

"I know." I laughed as if her barbs didn't make me want to body slam her. Although, if my wrestling moves looked anything like my tennis skills, that wouldn't end well. "I'm sure it's been interesting having his mother around."

"Yes, Mrs. Perkins is such a *sweet* lady, and she's been a *big* help to Cal while he's moving into Beverly Alspaugh's old house."

Mrs. Perkins? Sweet lady? Obviously, Taryn had never met Yvonne Conner. Interesting. It was also apparent she thought she was giving me the scoop about Cal's house. "He'll make a great neighbor."

Taryn flashed a fake smile.

"All right. Break's over." Kimberlee clapped her hands.

We climbed on our bikes, and I steeled myself for round two. Then, my phone chirped. I snatched it, launched myself off the bike, and hightailed it into the hall on shaky limbs. I didn't recognize the number and didn't care if it was a robocall. I'd pretend it was important.

"Georgia Winston."

"This is Yvonne."

"Hey! What's up?" I collapsed on a wooden bench and leaned my head against the wall.

"You and I need to talk—ASAP. I'd suggest we meet at that kooky little coffee shop, but seeing as how the owner kicked you out, that's off the table." There was no mistaking her irritation.

Was Yvonne put out with Bobbi Sue or me? "Bobbi Sue apologized and lifted my ban, so if you want to meet there we could, which is great because it's my favorite place around, and I didn't know what I was going to do if I couldn't get my caffeine fix—"

"Yea or nay on Latte Conspiracies?"

"What's this about?" I ran my hand over the bench's slats.

"I'm not getting into it over the phone. Name the time and place."

Considering I didn't know the topic of this conversation, I wasn't sure I wanted to have this discussion in public—or within Bobbi Sue's earshot. "Seven-thirty? My house?"

"Perfect. Cal's got some church meeting tonight, so he'll have no idea. See you then." She disconnected.

I stared at my phone for a good thirty seconds before I recovered enough to hobble back into class.

---

By the time Kimberlee had dismissed everyone, my legs that had once felt like gelatin now throbbed.

As Makayla and I approached, Kimberlee pointed a finger at us. "Stay away from me. Both of you."

"What'd *we* do?" Makayla asked.

"If you didn't kill Elias, then you know who did. You were

talking to him Saturday night, and I couldn't get a hold of him afterward." She grabbed her phone from her bike's console and took a step back. "We're done here."

"Please wait. We *don't* know who murdered Elias." I said. "We feel terrible about what happened and want to find his killer."

Her bloodshot eyes flashed. "Why were you talking to him in his dressing room?"

"My roommate Quincy Ashbrook ran off early Saturday morning. Sometimes Georgia works with the sheriff's department, so she's helping me figure out why. Now we're afraid Quincy's disappearance could have something to do with Dr. Kurtz's murder," Makayla said.

"It probably does." Kimberlee folded her arms. "That girl is bad news. He lost his job because of his fling with her."

I glanced at Makayla, but she hung her head, refusing to meet my gaze. I hadn't wanted to be right about Elias lying.

Kimberlee flipped her curly ponytail over her shoulder. "Go ahead. Ask your questions."

"How long did you know Elias?" I asked.

"A year or so. He worked out here regularly, and we had a lot in common. I encouraged him to audition for *The Sound of Music*." She took a deep breath. "We went on a couple of dates and really clicked." Her chin trembled. "I thought we might have something special."

"I'm sorry."

"Thanks." Her voice cracked.

"Other than Elias telling you he lost his job because of Quincy, did he talk about her?" I asked.

"He mentioned her a few times since they both sold Tune. I did overhear him on the phone with her once. They had a falling out over money. From what I could tell, it sounded like she owed him and refused to pay him back. It really hurt him."

"Are you a fan of Tune?" Makayla asked.

"I used to be. Berceuse helps me sleep, but"—Kimberlee shifted and stared at her gray shoes that coordinated with her mint green workout attire—"I heard a rumor about the company this morning and don't know if it's true."

"What's that?" I tried not to sound too eager.

"Tune sells lots of legit products. But rumor has it they have a secret product line where buyers can purchase illegal performance enhancing drugs. You have to have a password."

"Do you know what it is?" I asked.

"No. I just overheard some guys trying to figure it out."

Did Quincy sell illegal products? Had Elias threatened to be a whistleblower? And what about Jonas? He sold Tune as well. I grabbed a Winston Family Farms business card from my purse, scribbled Detective Hawk's number on the back, and handed the card to Kimberlee. "Tell Detective Hawk at the sheriff's department about that as soon as possible. Her number's on the back."

"I will." She glanced at the card and stowed it in her bag. "I've been wondering all day if the secret products have something to do with Elias's murder."

Or Quincy's disappearance. "Did anything else strange happen before Elias died?" I asked. "Any weird conversations? Did he ever seem upset?"

She squinted up at the water stained ceiling tiles. "Yeah. There was one odd thing—last Wednesday. I didn't think much about it at the time, but now . . ." She unearthed a thin sweatshirt from her workout bag on the floor. "I came in before our show and went to my dressing room like usual, and I saw him talking to two guys in his dressing room. He thanked them for thinking of him, but he couldn't do that." She slipped on the sweatshirt.

"Do what?" Makayla leaned forward.

Kimberlee shoved her hands in her pockets. "I wish I knew, but that's all I heard. Obviously, I only caught the end of the conversation, but I remember thinking it was weird. It was like they were selling something, but we *never* have salespeople back in our dressing rooms. Besides, the doors were locked, so Elias would've had to let them in. Now I'm wondering if they were after the illegal Tune products."

"Can you describe the guys?" I asked.

"Young. Early twenties. One had a reddish-colored beard— well, he was *trying* to grow a beard. The other kid had those 1980s glasses like creepers wear."

"Hang on a second." Makayla's fingers flew over her phone. "Are they in this picture?" She turned her phone and pointed at a picture of Jonas with a group of guys.

"Yeah. That's him." Kimberlee leaned closer. "And the kid in the glasses standing next to him is his buddy."

## CHAPTER FOURTEEN

"I s that guy with Jonas the one you went on the pick-a-date with?" I asked Makayla on the way out of Fitness Universe. The afternoon sunshine had disappeared along with the warmth, so in spite of my aching legs, I didn't dawdle.

"Yeah. Micah Bradford. He lives in the same house as Jonas and Aidan."

I unlocked my truck. "What do you know about him?" We got in, and I started the engine and cranked up the heat.

"He's a music education major from Nashville, and he and Jonas have a band called Brotherhood Road." Makayla buckled her seatbelt.

I snapped mine in place. "We know Jonas sells Tune. Maybe he was trying to let Elias in on the secret product line."

"But why would he have Micah with him? He doesn't sell Tune."

"Unless Micah uses the secret products. Does he work out a lot?"

"I'm not sure. He's definitely not ripped like Jonas. Aidan

posted a picture of the guys at a pool party. I'll see if I can find him so we can talk to him."

"It's good to know your stalking paid off."

"Like you never stalk men online." Her stomach rumbled, and she pointed to it. "Feed me."

I laughed. "What do you want?"

She scrunched up her face. "Chinese food."

"Perfect." I put my truck in gear. "I'm all about obliterating calorie deficits with orange chicken."

---

Makayla and I were cleaning up dinner when my phone rang, and I glanced at the display. *Mom.* I had about fifteen minutes to deal with this interruption before Yvonne was scheduled to show. I looked at my stepsister. "My mom wants to video chat. You did tell them what happened, right?"

Makayla refused to meet my gaze. She tipped a plate toward Gus, so he could lick it before she loaded it in the dishwasher. "Uh-oh. It sort of slipped my mind."

Right. And I had a million bucks sitting in a bank account that I'd forgotten about. Maybe I should give her the benefit of the doubt. With all the chaos, I hadn't remembered to check if she'd told them. I walked into the living room and collapsed in Daddy's old leather recliner next to the fireplace. "Hey, Mom. How are things going?"

Makayla hovered between the living room and kitchen out of sight of the camera.

"Wonderful. We wanted to check in. Is everything okay?" She tucked a strand of hair behind her ear and turned the camera toward Dan, who waved.

As far as she knew, why wouldn't things be okay? Either her mother's intuition was at work, or she'd heard something. "Yeah.

It's great. Getting ready for planting." That part was completely true.

"Good. Listen, we've been where we didn't have internet, but when we got to our hotel this evening, Dan had an email from Brenneman University. Quincy Ashbrook disappeared at the beginning of the chorale tour, so they cancelled it. Then we saw a news story that a former Brenneman professor had been killed. Anyway, Dan's worried because he hasn't heard from Makayla."

"Well, I thought she was going to call and tell you, but she's staying with me." I stood and crossed the room.

Dan sat next to Mom. "Why?"

I turned the camera toward Makayla.

"Hey, Dad. Jill." She explained what Quincy had done and that we were trying to find her.

"I see. Did you know the professor who was killed?" Mom asked.

"Yes. I took voice lessons from him."

"Do you think his murder has anything to do with Quincy taking off?" Dan furrowed his brow.

Makayla chewed her lip. "We don't know."

"That's not what I wanted to hear," Dan said. "We should move up our flight—"

"Dad, Georgia and I are fine. We're having fun. Besides, she has a security system."

"I know. I had it installed. So how did Quincy sneak out?" He eyed me.

Nothing got past Dan, but he'd had a lot of practice ferreting out the truth, raising his ornery twin sons. "I turned it off because Quincy triggered it earlier in the evening when she opened a window. She told me she was hot, and I believed her. We had above-normal temperatures that day."

"Well, don't do that again," Mom said.

"I won't." I tried not to sound annoyed. "How's your trip going?"

"Wonderful. We'll fill you in when we get home," Dan said. "Now, I'd feel a lot better if you'd go stay at our house until we're back. Our neighbors can look out for you."

Makayla nudged my foot, which I took to mean *no way*.

I gave her a thumbs up. "We're fine. If it makes you feel any better, Cal moved into Beverly's house."

Mom and Dan looked at each other, and seconds ticked by.

Dan glanced at his watch. "We need to meet our team, so we have to go. I'd still prefer you go to Richardville, but you're adults. I trust you'll make a wise decision."

I was convinced he'd earned a masters in guilt-trip studies. "I appreciate that."

Makayla stepped out of camera view so she could roll her eyes.

Even though Dan had left the final decision up to us, as we said goodbye and disconnected, I had a gut feeling this matter wasn't settled.

---

"I'll bet you've been racking your brain ever since I called." Yvonne burst through my front door later that night and stared at me. "Cal's told me how much you like to solve mysteries." She slipped off her leopard-print trench coat and held it out.

"Yes." I placed her coat on the bench. "Let's have a seat in the living room."

Makayla had gone upstairs with Gus, but I wondered if she was in the hall eavesdropping instead of hiding in her room. I wouldn't blame her one bit.

"Hard at work on the Quincy Ashbrook case, I see." Yvonne pointed at my dining room wall as she passed.

I needed to make a chalk wall for my office, where I could shut the door. "My stepsister is pretty upset since Quincy's her roommate. Plus, I feel responsible since she escaped my house." I led her into my living room and motioned to the two chairs arranged next to my piano.

"Can't blame you there, but you'd better be careful. I told Cal and Vanessa, that girl's up to no good. Wouldn't surprise me one bit if she was the one who killed Elias Kurtz."

"But they don't think she did?"

"Nice try." Yvonne crossed her thin legs that were made for the black skinny jeans she was wearing. "My son is tight-lipped, and he's taking some time off. Wouldn't surprise me if the girl did it, though, but that's the detective in me speculating. I may've retired, but my curiosity didn't. What do *you* think happened?"

I didn't have a great theory yet, but I couldn't admit that to Yvonne. Her laser-like eyes blinked with impatience.

*Start talking, Georgia Rae.* "Well, Quincy, her ex-boyfriend Jonas, and Elias Kurtz may've been selling illegal performance enhancing drugs under the cover of a legitimate nutritional supplement company. Elias may've been planning to blow the whistle, and it got him killed." As I said the words, I realized that idea wasn't half-bad.

"Don't have much, do you?"

Scratch that. "No, ma'am. It's not my job."

"Fair enough. You sure your stepsister ain't involved?"

"Yes. I'm sure." I curled my fingers around the chair's arm.

"How?" She flicked her pointy black pump off and then back onto her heel.

"I just am." I cringed inwardly. *Good grief.* I sounded like Makayla. "Why'd you want to talk? I doubt it has anything to do with Quincy Ashbrook."

"Right to the point. You and I are going to get along fine." She pressed her elbows into the chair arms, and her gold bangle bracelets dinged as she steepled her fingers. "Mason Thrailkill. Tell me what you know."

"He and Cal were both detectives when Cal worked in Ohio."

"And?"

What'd she want me to say? Cal had mentioned Mason a few times, but I'd never met him. "Mason's name was written on a sticky note on Vanessa's computer monitor. Mason probably has something to do with why you visited Vanessa behi—without Cal knowing." I met her gaze. "I haven't had time to figure out what."

"I'll save you the trouble since you're already busy poking around another case." She rested her hands in her lap. "Mason Thrailkill's wife Natalie was stabbed to death last month while she was riding her bike."

I shuddered. "That's awful."

"It is. Mason and Natalie spent a lot of time with Cal. Went to the same church and all. She was as nice as they come."

"Was she raped?" I could hardly bring myself to ask the question.

"No, thankfully she didn't have to endure that horror. At first, the police thought she was in the wrong place at the wrong time —that some sicko killer was trolling for the next victim and Natalie was it. Then, a week later Mason got a note that said, 'How does it feel? You killed the person I loved. And now I've taken the one you love.'"

My heart somersaulted. "Did Mason kill someone in the line of duty?"

"No, but they've zeroed in on two cases Mason worked where suspects died. One was stabbed in prison while awaiting trial for murder. The other had a heart attack while under investigation. In both instances, they later found evidence exonerating the suspects."

My mind whirred. "Did Cal work on the same cases?"

"The one where the prime suspect had a heart attack."

"He never told me any of this." I wrapped my arms around my waist.

"I know." She pressed her lips together. "Somehow, my son convinced himself that what happened to Mason's wife might happen to you, and he didn't want to put you in danger."

"He told you that?"

"Nope."

"Then how do you know?"

"Did my son pull away?"

"Yes."

"Did he give you a good reason?"

"Not really." *Is this what an interrogation feels like?*

"Did he claim he was going through something but didn't give you specifics?"

"Yes."

"Were you frustrated enough by his emotional distance to break up with him?"

"Yes."

"Then what more do you need to know?"

*That he loves me.* I shook away the thought. Something else was bothering me—big time. "If that's true, then why would Cal go on a date with Taryn? Wouldn't he want to protect *her* from a nutcase?"

"*She* asked *him* out—I read their text messages." She waved a hand. "Persistent little gal," she muttered.

*Merciful heavens.* I should tell Cal to change his passcode.

"He's trying to get over you," Yvonne said. "He's not into Taryn. He went on a date with her to get her off his back and because now we're not certain that Mason's case has anything to do with Cal."

"He told you?"

"Nope."

137

"Then how do you know?"

"Are you suggesting I don't know my own son?"

Why, oh why, had I jumped on this merry-go-round again? "No."

"Are you doubting that I'm not seeing that old sparkle in his eyes ever since you two broke up?"

"No."

"Then what more do you need to know?"

"Is Mason the reason he's taking time off?"

"Sure is. That and the move."

The move was a convenient excuse for everyone except his mother. I squeezed the bridge of my nose. "Yvonne, this information is helpful, but what do you want me to do?"

"They say men marry women like their mothers."

I'd never experienced conversational whiplash quite like this before. I rubbed the back of my neck. *Find an insurance code for that one, Doc.*

"I've heard." I nearly choked on the words.

"You and me?" She pointed at me and then herself. "We're doers." She leaned back and folded her arms. "It's why I can't keep my nose out of my son's love life and why you can't stay out of his investigations."

That wasn't completely accurate. "I can't help that I've found—"

"Does Yvonne sound like she's done?"

*Georgia wishes she were.* "No, ma'am."

"You and me also like to fix things. Now I'm pretty good with a hammer and nails—used to drive Darrell nuts that I could repair things better than him. His ego couldn't take it." She sniffed. "Anyway, I was a tomboy growing up, always following my daddy around."

My face began to simmer because that scenario sounded a little too familiar. Would I be like Yvonne in thirty years?

"When Yvonne sees a situation that needs to be repaired, she goes in and does what she can." She stood.

I hoisted myself out of the chair and warred against an emerging grimace. *Stupid cycling class.* "Good for you." And here I'd thought she'd come to help Cal move into his house. *Silly me.* "I do have one more question though."

"Sure."

"Why were you talking to Detective Hawk earlier today?"

She draped her arm over my shoulder as we headed for my front door. "Because if she's any kind of cop, she's got Cal's back, but I was willing to bet my pension she didn't have the full story about Mason."

"Did she?"

"Nope. She knew about his wife passing, but that was it." She gave me a squeeze. "I set her straight because I need her on my team while I'm fixing things with you and Cal."

## CHAPTER FIFTEEN

I growled and drove my fist into my pillow. Thanks to Yvonne's visit, sleep was nowhere in sight. I flopped back on my bed and stared at the ceiling.

Yvonne wanted to fix my relationship with Cal—as if it were up to her. Knowing what had been bothering him helped, but not much. Why couldn't he have told me about Mason and Natalie? Instead, he'd shut me out and said his life wasn't a mystery for me to solve. Why would he think I'd try to solve a case in another state that didn't even involve me? Why would he assume Mason and Natalie's situation would happen to him? What about trusting God with the future?

Maybe I hadn't been patient enough with Cal. I covered my face with my hands. No. I hadn't felt at peace about our relationship, so I'd ended things.

I rolled on my side. Not to mention, Hamlet added another layer of complication. I really liked him and wanted to get to know him better. I hoped he felt the same, but I wasn't sure since he'd told me he didn't want to be my rebound relationship. What if that was just an excuse?

"God," I whispered. "I don't know what to do. Are you showing me there's still hope with Cal? Should I give Hamlet a chance? Is there someone else out there? Or maybe I'm just supposed to be single forever." I fluffed my pillow. "Please show me your will . . . and help me sleep."

---

"I figured out where we can find Micah Bradford," Makayla said the next morning.

We were scarfing down Frosted Flakes at my kitchen table. Gus perched between us, moving his head back and forth and keeping an eye out for rogue cereal pieces.

After getting a few hours of sleep, it took me a minute to remember who she was talking about. *Jonas's friend and bandmate. Look alive, Georgia Rae.* "Where?"

"He's in Richardville."

My spoon clinked against the bowl. "Seriously?"

"Yep. I stalked his social media last night. He's student teaching at Hillside Elementary, and they aren't on spring break until next week."

I sipped my coffee and formed a plan. "I need to set up measurements for planting, but I could take a break to stakeout the school parking lot this afternoon. Maybe he'll talk to us."

"Sounds good." She shrieked and dropped her spoon.

Coffee slopped onto my pajamas. "Ow!" I dabbed my lap with a napkin. "What?"

She pointed behind me, and I faced the door where her identical twin brothers were peering through the window and making faces.

I hadn't had enough caffeine to deal with them, but I tossed my napkin aside and let them in. "To what do we owe the pleasure of this visit?" I looked back and forth between the blond pair who'd nicknamed themselves the Twin Menaces—and who were as handsome as they believed. I was getting better at telling them apart and didn't need to rely on the scar underneath Austin's eye the way I once had.

"We heard Mak is your sidekick this week." Preston patted Gus on the head.

"And that you're investigating Quincy's vanishing act." Austin squared his broad shoulders and crossed his arms.

Uh-oh. There was only one way they'd learned all this information, and I had a bad feeling about what was coming.

*Wait for it . . .*

"Dad and Jill asked us to stay with you." Preston smirked. "Jill says you have plenty of space."

Makayla groaned and buried her face in her arms.

*Wait . . . what?* I blinked at them. I'd expected a demand for sidekick action. How naïve was I? "I have a security system."

That excuse had sounded better in my head.

"Sissy." Austin puffed out his chest. "Presty and I are *way* better than any security system."

In spite of being annoying, they'd both played football for Richardville High School, and at twenty-five they kept their hulking figures in shape, which could come in handy. "Well, I—"

"Cool!" Austin gave Preston a high five, and if they hadn't been wearing shirts and ties for their work as real estate agents, I would've expected them to bump chests.

Makayla lifted her head and gaped at them.

"Tell us where to put our stuff. We need to get to work." Preston opened the back door and dragged in two large suitcases with garment bags draped over them.

How was this happening?

I shot Makayla a helpless glance, but she'd simply resumed eating her cereal. Apparently, she knew when to surrender.

"How long are you expecting to stay?" I stared at the luggage. "I wouldn't take that monstrosity of a bag for a week's vacation."

"A few days. You know we have to look good at all times," Preston said. "Do you have spare keys?"

I grabbed the back of a chair and held on for dear life. Preston had been showing teeny glimmers of maturity, and I'd broken him of the habit of calling me *babe*. But the thought of the boys having unrestricted access to my house actually made me dizzy. "I don't have them lying around because Mom has one, and Brandi and Ashley have keys, and so does my Grandpa, but that's it. So I guess you'll have to make sure I'm here. Even Dakota doesn't have a key, which makes sense since he's an hour away and—"

"Presty." Austin elbowed his brother. "We don't need keys. Don't you remember?"

"Dude, that's right. I completely forgot."

My eyes widened. "Why don't you need keys?"

"Two years ago, at Dad and Jill's Memorial Day cookout, we stole your keyring and had duplicates made in case we wanted to prank you." Austin fished a key out of his pocket and jiggled it. "That was before we decided we like you." He winked.

Preston turned to me. "We're good then. Just give us the code for your alarm system."

---

Pick-up at Hillside Elementary School ended a little past three o'clock, so Makayla and I cruised the lot searching for a vehicle with a Brenneman University parking pass like the one on her Prius's rear window.

We'd waited at a safe distance until traffic cleared, because past experience had taught me it wasn't safe to be within a close radius of any elementary school after dismissal. The way some parents zoomed out of the lot made me think they'd been the ones trapped inside all day with only one recess.

"There it is." Makayla pointed at a beat-up Honda. I eased into the space next to the car.

"I hope he doesn't stay here working for hours." I cracked the windows and shut off my truck.

"No kidding." She studied her phone.

"Georgia Rae! Makayla! What're you doing?" Hamlet waved as he approached the truck.

My face burned as I opened my window more and snuck a quick peek at Makayla, who was giving us her full attention. "Were you subbing today?" I managed to sound halfway cool, considering I probably looked as red as the playground slide across the way.

"Yes. I tried my hand as a fifth-grade teacher." He shook his head. "I'd rather work with middle and high school students in Wildcat Springs, but I survived."

He'd been taking substitute teaching jobs at local schools to fund his house flip.

"What are *you* doing?" Hamlet-the-Persistent asked again.

"We're waiting on one of Makayla's friends to come out because we have a few questions about Quincy." I fixed my eyes on the door. "He's a student teacher here."

"I see." He leaned against my truck. "I'm glad I ran into you because I've been meaning to call."

The door to the main entrance opened, and Micah strolled out of the building. He hadn't lost the retro glasses, and he sported a Mr. Rogers-like cardigan.

I held up one finger. "We'll talk after Makayla and I are done. Excuse us."

Makayla and I hopped out and waited on the sidewalk in front of the truck, but Hamlet didn't leave my side.

Makayla waved. "Micah?"

He approached us. "Hey, Mak. What's going on?"

"We need to talk about Quincy Ashbrook," she said.

"Okay?" He squinted at Hamlet and me.

I smiled. "I'm Georgia—Makayla's stepsister." I motioned toward Hamlet. "And this is my friend Hamlet."

"Nice to meet you." He shifted his navy backpack to his opposite shoulder and glanced toward his car. "Could we make this quick? I'm kind of in a hurry."

"Sure." I sensed the need for a friendly approach, so I kept my tone pleasant. "I don't know if you've heard, but Quincy disappeared last weekend, and then Dr. Kurtz—a former Brenneman professor—was murdered."

His face remained expressionless. "Yeah. Weird situation—and sad."

"Makayla's been worried about Quincy, and we've been talking to people who know her to see if they have any idea why she left."

"You think *I* know something about that crazy chick?" He scoffed. "Lady, I've been student teaching all semester. It's consuming my life." He turned toward his car.

Hamlet stiffened, and I had a feeling he was about ten seconds away from putting this kid in his place.

"I understand. I went through student teaching myself," I said. "But since you're friends with Jonas, we thought you might remember something—anything—that might help."

He pushed up his glasses. "First of all, Jo and Q broke up, and I say good riddance."

*Interesting take.* Jonas had made the split sound amicable. "What happened?" I asked.

"She lost interest in Jo. Could've been seeing someone else." Micah glanced at his watch.

I peeked at Makayla, who had her arms crossed. "Elias Kurtz?"

"No. But I heard rumors about them a couple of years ago."

"How do you know Quincy wasn't seeing Elias?" I asked.

"I straight up asked Jo."

"How would he know?" Makayla asked.

"Q must've told him." He scowled. "Here's the thing. Jo and I never would've asked Elias to be the lead singer in our band if he'd been dating Q. We don't need the drama."

I remembered what Kimberlee Samson had told us. "Did this conversation take place at Bell's Dinner Theater?"

He frowned. "Yeah."

I charged ahead before he got skittish. "Why ask Elias?"

"That guy could sing. He was classically trained, but he has an awesome country sound." He turned to Makayla. "Remember when he sang that song he wrote at Brenneman's talent show and everybody went crazy?"

"Yeah. It was great." Her cheeks turned pink, and she ducked her head.

*Moving on.* "What'd Elias say when you asked him?"

"He thanked us and turned us down. Said life on the road wasn't for him. See, Jo was freaking out because his brother got us a gig opening for Parker Curtis this summer. But we lost our lead singer last month, so we were pretty desperate. We found somebody else though, so it's all good." Micah grinned. "We're all moving to Nashville after graduation. My grandma said we can live in her garage apartment rent free if we do handyman stuff for her. We've given ourselves two years to make it in the music business, and then we'll start our fallback careers." He looked at his watch again. "I've got to go."

I nodded. "One quick thing. What do you know about Tune Nutritional Supplements?"

He turned up his nose. "Quincy and Jonas sold the stuff. I tried one of Jo's sample packets, the kind you mix in water, and it made me gag. Definitely not my thing."

As far as I could tell, his words and reaction seemed sincere. "Thanks for your time."

Micah rushed to his car, and I turned to Hamlet, who was staring at Micah.

"He may need to give himself more time to achieve his dream," he said.

Interesting takeaway. "Do you regret leaving acting?"

He shook his head. "I'll always be an actor, and if a show comes along that I'm interested in, I'll audition at Bell's or for other local companies. But I've had my fill of moving around, and I don't have a desire to pursue film or TV."

Makayla snuck away to the playground and sat on a bench next to a teeter-totter, proving she was more mature than her brothers, who would've stuck around listening just to torture me.

"What'd you want to talk to me about?" My heart fluttered—a teeny bit.

"I've been thinking about our conversation the other day, and I made an error in judgement."

My cheeks warmed. "I'm sorry about the kiss—"

"I don't regret that. However, I never should've decided for you that you aren't ready to move past your relationship with Detective Perkins. I should've asked you on a date and let you decide for yourself."

"I see." I flipped my braid between my fingers. How honest should I be? "The thing is—you were right about me still struggling with my feelings for Cal. I wish it weren't the case, but it's been really hard."

He rested a hand on my shoulder. "I get it. It took me a while to get over my last relationship, but God helped me see my ex-girlfriend wasn't his best."

"Thanks for understanding. I care about you, and I don't want to hurt you."

"I know." He studied me, and I squirmed under his scrutiny. "Perhaps I have a solution," he said.

"What's that?"

"I'm content with my life right now. I'm building a new business, and no one else has caught my attention the way you have, Georgia Rae." He squeezed my shoulder and then dropped his hand to his side. "I'll gladly give you time to heal and pray for God's guidance."

I couldn't expect him to wait forever, but it was a generous—and kind—offer. "Okay—I have been."

"Excellent." He grinned. "When you're ready, say the magic words, and I'll whisk you away on a date."

"And what if I'm not?"

"Then we'll trust God to make that clear to both of us."

Peace flooded over me. "That sounds good. Thank you for understanding." I reached out and squeezed his hand.

"You're worth it, Georgia Rae." He kissed my cheek. "Have a wonderful evening." He strode over to his new truck.

Makayla jogged toward me as Hamlet drove out of the parking lot. "Did he ask you out?"

"Sort of."

"What does that mean?"

I told her.

"Wow. He *really* likes you."

"I know."

# CHAPTER SIXTEEN

Not long after Makayla and I had returned home from talking to Micah, my phone chirped with a text message from Brandi.

I'm on my way with dinner.

My best friend knew me well, and since she was on spring break, she must've had some extra time on her hands. I never turned down an offer of free food.

Ten minutes later, she was at my front door with her crockpot in hand and a grocery bag slung over her arm.

I took the crockpot from her and led her to the kitchen. "Mom and Dan ordered the Twin Menaces to stay with us," I whispered as I set her slow cooker on the counter and plugged it in.

Brandi slid the bag off her arm and set it on the table. "Then it's a good thing I made extra."

I lifted the crock pot's lid and peered inside. "What've you got there?" The fragrant soup filled the kitchen with a taco-like scent.

"Chicken tortilla soup." She took a container of homemade chocolate chip cookies and a package of tortilla chips from the bag. "And why *are* the boys staying with you?"

"To protect us."

"Fun." She laughed.

"It's always an adventure with the Winston-Farthing family." I ripped open the bag of chips. "How was the Parker Curtis concert?" I popped a chip in my mouth.

"Amazing. We had the best time." She took her phone out of her purse and showed me pictures of her and her sister with Parker. "He even signed T-shirts for us."

"That's great." I grinned. "Now, the Georgia Rae Winston Sensor detected chemistry between you and Lukas Dawes. What's the story?"

"We were friends—mostly freshman year. He started in education before he changed his major to music business. It was nice to see him again."

"You seemed more excited than just *nice* the other night."

"I did, didn't I?" She twisted her beaded bracelet. "I admit, I thought we could reconnect, but I don't think that's going to happen."

"Why not? He looked happy to see you."

"He was, but when Carly and I saw him at the concert, he was in business mode. It's pretty clear his whole life is the Parker Curtis Band. It just seems like he's changed." She shrugged. "I still had a great time. I mean, I met Parker Curtis for crying out loud!"

Preston, who'd changed into black athletic shorts and a Purdue T-shirt, sauntered into the kitchen and swept an appreciative gaze over Brandi. "Hey, there. Preston Farthing." He held out his hand. "Do I smell tacos?"

"Tortilla soup." She grinned as she looked up at him and shook his hand.

"Now that's a name I've never heard." His eyes gleamed.

Her cheeks turned pink, and she tucked a stray curl behind her ear. "It's Brandi. I *made* the tortilla soup."

"We certainly appreciate it, Brandi. I see you know my stepsister well, and if it depended on her to feed us, we'd starve." He flung his arm around my shoulder and gave it a squeeze.

Brandi put her hands on her hips. "She's invited us over plenty of times, and we've never gone hungry."

"Sure. As long as there are restaurants in town. But what if there's a zombie apocalypse, and they all shut down?" He peeked inside the cookie container and slid one out. "What then?"

"Then I have a well-stocked pantry I'm willing to share." She crossed her arms.

"Oh? I'll consider that an open invitation to your house." He winked and bit into the cookie.

She'd walked right into that trap before I could stop her.

"That'd be perfect." Her eyes danced. "I'll send you out to protect us from the zombies."

*What's happening right now?*

"Protection is my specialty." He grinned and flexed his arm muscles. "Are you going to stay and eat with us?" He shoved the remainder of the cookie in his mouth.

There was no mistaking the hopefulness in his tone. *Good grief.*

"I should get home."

He swallowed. "Have you eaten?"

"Not yet."

I could've sworn I detected more eye-batting from my friend, but with the stress of the last few days, it was possible I was hallucinating. What was with her lately?

"Then I insist. You *made* the food. You should definitely stay and enjoy it with us." He turned to me. "Right, Georgia?"

"Yes. Please stay."

"I'd love to," she said.

"Awesomesauce. Your cookies are great, by the way. I'll go get Austy and Mak." Preston bounded out of my kitchen, and Gus scuttled behind him.

"Sorry about that." I took a stack of bowls from my cabinet and handed them to Brandi.

"Why?"

"You have to ask?"

She began setting the kitchen table. "Georgia, do you know how long it's been since a guy has flirted with me?"

"You've been on dates." I pulled five soup spoons out of my utensil drawer.

"Sure, but in case you've forgotten, Jon Nordmeyer is one of the most serious guys I've ever met."

"True." After my stepdad had fixed me up with Jon and it hadn't worked out, I'd introduced him to Brandi, which hadn't been a successful match either. "What about Dalton?"

"He has a decent sense of humor, and we had some nice dates." She folded a napkin and tucked it next to the bowl.

"But he doesn't flirt."

"Right. At least—not with me, so I don't think he's going to call again." She lowered her voice. "Look. Your step-brothers are what? Thirteen? Fourteen years younger than me?"

"Yeah. They just turned twenty-five."

She nodded. "If a handsome twenty-five-year-old guy wants to flirt with me, I'm flattered, and it's harmless. In fact, it gives me hope that I'm not a shriveled up old woman and still have what it takes to attract a man." She leaned against a chair. "I know that sounds pathetic, but—"

"It doesn't." *But please, please, pretty please don't date Preston.* I couldn't bear to think of how badly he'd treat her.

"Relax. It's no big deal." She looked at me as if she were reading my mind. Had years of teaching honed that trick?

"You're right." My voice sounded a little squeaky. "He's just a flirt."

Preston burst into the kitchen and flashed a huge smile at Brandi. "Let's eat!"

I took a bit of consolation in one small fact. At least he wasn't calling her babe—yet.

---

After dinner, Preston insisted on playing Chinese checkers. I interpreted this as a thinly veiled excuse for spending more time with Brandi. She agreed to stay since she didn't have school the next morning, so we gathered around my dining room table and placed the colored marbles on the wooden board.

I sat next to Austin, facing the chalkboard so I could ponder the case while we played. He nudged me and pointed at the wall. "What does Tune have to do with Quincy and the professor who was killed?"

"Do you use their products?" I asked.

"Presty and I both do."

"I'm into Vivace. I don't even need caffeine," Preston said.

Brandi grinned. "Let me guess. It helps you wake up and be lively."

"You know it." He winked.

I fought the urge to barf in my mouth.

"You never answered my question, sissy." Austin rolled a black marble between his fingers.

"When are you going to stop calling Georgia *sissy*?" Makayla asked. "She's your elder. You should be more respectful."

"A thousand pardons." Austin placed the marble on the board and pressed his hands together. "You haven't answered my question, oh wise, elder sister."

Preston looked as if he was about to explode trying to tamp down his laughter—which I assumed was part of his ongoing effort to prove his maturity to Brandi.

Brandi giggled—seriously an authentic school-girl *giggle*.

*Welcome to the Winston-Farthing Circus.* "Quincy and her ex-boyfriend Jonas are distributors. So was the former professor who was murdered. Then, we heard Tune has a secret product line of illegal performance enhancing drugs that people can get if they have a password." I looked back and forth between my step-brothers. "Have you ever heard anything like this?"

Preston shook his head. "No. I always thought Tune was legit. My buddy Conrad's never offered me any performance enhancing drugs." Underneath his fitted T-shirt, his pecs flexed. "Yep. Probably knows I don't need it."

Makayla and I groaned.

"Same here." Austin's eyes gleamed. "But you don't happen to know the password, do you?"

"No." Then it hit me. *Musical terms. Tempo. Chord. Berceuse. Vivace.* I turned to Makayla. "Remember the scrap I found in your room?

Her eyes widened. "What if Forza 12 is the secret password?"

"Want me to call Conrad and see if he knows?" Austin asked.

"Yes," I said.

"Dude, you think Conrad's into the shady stuff?" Preston asked.

"If there's a secret, Conrad's in the know."

"Are you sure this isn't dangerous?" Brandi asked.

"No. But we'll be careful." Austin had already dialed and put his phone to his ear. "Connie, my man! Sup?" He listened. "I got

Presty here with me. You cool on speaker?" Austin set his phone on the table. "Look, Presty and I want to build more muscle to impress the chicks, you know?"

"Sure do." Conrad's voice reverberated through my dining room. "Want me to order you some Beat Protein Shakes?"

"Actually, I heard I should ask about the Forza 12 products."

We all looked around the table while we waited for Conrad to answer. Instead, a guffaw boomed across the line.

"Dude, I don't know where you heard that, but that's an urban legend."

## CHAPTER SEVENTEEN

"I shoulda known my buddy Trevor didn't know what he was talking about." Austin huffed with fake indignation.

"No worries," Conrad said. "Years ago, one of our competitors made up that story to discredit the company. Every so often I have somebody ask about Forza 12. Look, I hope you ain't thinking about getting into the illegal stuff, man."

"No. I'll be straight with you. Presty and I are helping our stepsister with an investigation, and—"

"The tall, hot one who's the farmer-detective?"

I pressed my hands against my face. I'd never met Conrad, so I didn't even want to think about where he'd gotten his information.

"Yeah. The farmer-detective." Austin stuck his finger in his throat, and Makayla swatted his arm. "She had a tip about the Forza 12 products," he said.

"Search for it on one of those urban-legend busting websites, and you'll see there's nothing to it," Conrad said.

Brandi picked up her phone and typed.

"Will do. Thanks for your help, and go ahead and order me a case of the protein shakes."

"Me too," Preston said.

"Sure thing. Catch you guys later."

Austin disconnected, leaned back, and folded his arms across his chest. "Admit it. I make an awesome sidekick."

"Good work, Austy." Preston high-fived him.

"Conrad's right," Brandi said. "Forza 12 is an urban legend, though they've never proven which competitor started the rumor. Ten years ago, there was a federal investigation into the company, and it's completely above board."

I squeezed the bridge of my nose. Now that we knew Tune was a legitimate company, my most promising lead had evaporated.

---

After tossing and turning for half the night while I considered other possible reasons for Quincy's disappearance as well as my drama with Hamlet and Cal, I awakened the next morning, found Dr. Jackson's card, and gave him a call. He agreed to meet at Brenneman's student center later that morning.

Makayla and I decided it would be best if I handled this interview on my own, since she didn't want to risk upsetting him. Still, she came along for the ride.

When we arrived on campus, the sun finally came out of hiding, and we hurried along the daffodil-lined sidewalk to the Korman Student Center. Once we were inside, Makayla disappeared into the bookstore. The building had a large atrium with a bear-shaped fountain in the center and a food court surrounding it. Since the college was on spring break, the only place open was Bear's Brews Coffee Shop.

Dr. Jackson sat at a table nearly obscured by a massive fern, and there were a few other people spaced throughout the large area. He was sipping from an oversized mug and working at a laptop. Even though he was supposed to be on vacation, he wore a shirt and tie with piano keyboard print.

"Thank you for seeing me." I pulled out a chair and sat.

"You're welcome." He closed his laptop. "I apologize for getting so upset with you over Miss Ashbrook's stunt. You were certainly not to blame."

"Everyone was stressed that morning."

"Yes." He removed his wire-rimmed glasses and placed them on the table. "How may I help?"

"I'm looking for clarification. Was Elias Kurtz's contract not renewed because he had a relationship with Quincy Ashbrook?"

He met my gaze and didn't blink. "Yes."

I hadn't expected Dr. Jackson to answer so freely.

"One of my colleagues mentioned seeing Elias and Miss Ashbrook together outside of school during the spring semester of her sophomore year. When I spoke with Elias, he claimed the meeting was for the Tune Nutritional Supplement business. I believed him, but a month later, when Mr. Ashbrook came to me with evidence that his daughter was involved with Elias, we had no choice but to let Elias go."

The Ashbrooks had lied—or at least Mr. Ashbrook had lied. "Where'd he get the evidence?"

"My impression was that he hired a private investigator. He certainly has the means."

"Did Quincy's father believe getting rid of Elias would stop them from seeing each other? If anything, it would give them a legitimate excuse to be together since he no longer worked for the school."

"I agree. But one simply does not argue with Stuart Ashbrook."

It was clear Dr. Jackson would be open as long as I asked the right questions. "Is Mr. Ashbrook in the habit of throwing his weight around?"

"In a manner of speaking, yes."

"How so?"

Dr. Jackson took a sip from his mug. "I shouldn't say." But he looked like he wanted to tell me something. The fountain's trickling water infused the growing silence.

I barged ahead. "Did Stuart Ashbrook offer you a financial incentive to ensure Quincy's acceptance to Brenneman?"

"Miss Ashbrook earned the music department's recommendation based entirely on her audition." He nodded slowly as if he were trying to send a clear message. "She has a lovely voice and a talent for music composition. I gave her name to admissions because she earned it. What happened after that was out of my hands." He laced his fingers. "*My* conscience and bank account are completely clear."

"You weren't kidding when you said the Ashbrooks are hands on."

"No, I most certainly was not. For example, Mrs. Ashbrook manages most of her daughter's Tune business, though I'm not sure Mr. Ashbrook is aware."

"How'd you find that out?"

"Elias told me when he was trying to convince me his relationship with Miss Ashbrook was simply a business arrangement —and that he rarely saw her outside of school."

I was certain Stuart didn't know about Janet's help, because she'd pretended that Elias was simply Quincy's voice professor and the son of her college friend. If she helped Quincy, she definitely would've known Elias was part of her upline.

Dr. Jackson scooped up his laptop. "If you'll excuse me, I have another appointment, but please feel free to call if you have more questions."

As he strode away, I considered what he'd just told me.

Whatever was going on with Quincy, I was beginning to find it difficult to believe her parents didn't know—and weren't somehow involved.

———————

As soon as Dr. Jackson left, Makayla returned with two disposable coffee cups. "I got you a white chocolate mocha. It doesn't have a cool name like Bobbi Sue's drinks, but it's pretty good." She set the cups on the table and pulled out a chair.

I told her what Dr. Jackson had said about Stuart throwing his weight around and Janet handling Quincy's Tune business.

"I'm not surprised." Makayla twisted the cardboard ring on her cup.

"Why?"

"You know how we talked about Quincy not being a very good student?"

"Yeah."

"Quincy does fine in her music classes, but she gets by in the other required courses because her mom helps. She always edits Quincy's essays. Not just proofreading. Major rewriting. If Mrs. Ashbrook could come take tests for Quincy, she would."

"What about Mr. Ashbrook?"

"No way. He's more of a sink or swim kind of guy."

If Stuart didn't know about Janet managing the Tune business, was she hiding her help with Quincy's schoolwork too? I considered Janet's naïve reaction about Elias. Was Stuart keeping Janet in the dark about Quincy's relationship with Elias? If so, what did these secrets they were keeping say about the state of their marriage?

"Has Quincy ever said anything about her parents' relationship?" I asked.

"No. It's obvious Mr. Ashbrook likes control and is hard to

please, but they get along because Mrs. Ashbrook always seems like she lives in a giant bubble. At least from what I've seen." She shrugged. "Who knows? They could just be putting on a big show."

I wouldn't doubt that one bit.

———

That evening, I had to have something to feed my stepsiblings, and since I'd been calibrating my planter and working on tillage equipment all afternoon, Wednesday Night Wings at Pizza Heaven would be my lifeline. I drove into Wildcat Springs and waited almost half an hour at a swamped restaurant. I arrived home with honey barbeque wings, coleslaw, fries, and a growling stomach. My hand froze on the garage door opener. Makayla's car was gone.

Weird.

She hadn't mentioned going anywhere because she was working on an essay, and she knew I was bringing food.

As I walked inside the house, Gus howled and rattled in his crate. I checked my phone, but she hadn't texted. An inspection of the kitchen and living room showed she hadn't left a note.

I let Gus out and told myself to stop being so nervous. Makayla was a grown woman. If she needed to run an errand, she didn't need to check in like she was a kid, but after everything that'd happened, it would've been courteous if she'd told me.

I sent her a text.

I'm back at the house with supper.

I started to message Preston and Austin to ask about Makayla but stopped myself. They'd be home before too much longer. I needed to calm down, but I couldn't shake the uneasy feeling roiling in my gut.

After I tossed my purse in my bedroom and kicked off my shoes, I called her—and got voicemail.

"Argh! What is she thinking, Gus?"

He followed me back into the kitchen, dropped onto the floor, and gnawed a squeaky toy.

*So helpful.*

I was plunking silverware on the kitchen table with more force than necessary when Austin let himself into my back door and disarmed my security system. I'd already vowed to change the code when this ordeal was over.

"Please tell me you've heard from Makayla."

"No. Why?" He slipped out of his coat, tossed it on a chair, and loosened his tie.

"I went to pick up supper, and when I came back, she was gone. I have no idea where she went. She didn't even leave a note, and she hasn't answered my text or call."

"Bizarre." He tapped his phone and waited. "No answer."

"I know."

He jabbed at his phone and put it to his ear. "You talked to Mak this afternoon? She left without telling Georgia." He peeked in the Pizza Heaven sack, took out a fry, and shoved it in his mouth. "All right." He disconnected. "Presty hasn't heard from her either. He just finished a showing and will be here in ten." His fingers flew over his phone. "I'm bombarding her with annoying messages." He stuck out his tongue and snapped a selfie.

I wasn't sure how being annoying would help. "I'll check her room."

With Gus and Austin following, I had a major case of déjà vu as we trudged upstairs to investigate. This time, I entered my childhood bedroom instead of the guest room.

Makayla's laptop was closed on my old desk. She'd made the twin bed, and her suitcase was tucked in the closet. I strode to the bathroom and flipped on the lights, but only the toiletry bag rested on the counter.

Austin opened her laptop, and I peered at the computer screen. Makayla had been writing an essay comparing and contrasting Calvinism and Arminianism and had left off in the middle of a sentence. A photo minimized in the lower righthand corner caught my attention.

"Open that." I pointed at the icon.

Austin clicked, and a selfie of Makayla holding a piece of paper with typed words appeared. As I skimmed the message, my heart plunged to my feet.

# CHAPTER EIGHTEEN

I pressed my hand to my mouth and reread the message.

Makayla,

If you want to see your friend alive, put the broken file on Floyd Fillmore's grave at Fillmore Cemetery and leave immediately. You have until 6:00 today. No police or nosy stepsister or Quincy dies.

I gripped the edge of my desk to steady myself, trying to sort through everything we'd learned. Austin sat frozen with clenched fists.

Quincy's parents had been right all along. Sort of. Someone had kidnapped the girls—for a *file*? When Quincy hadn't been able to produce it, the kidnapper had turned to Makayla? What would Makayla have access to that was so valuable? I glanced at the clock. "It's 6:26. She should be home by now."

"I'll call her." He dialed and waited. "No answer." He muttered something unintelligible under his breath.

The back door slammed, and Gus woofed. Austin and I lunged toward the hallway.

"It's me," Preston yelled. "Where are you guys?"

"Upstairs. We've got a major problem." I sent the picture of the note to my phone.

Preston joined us, and we showed him the picture. He scowled. "Let's get to the cemetery. It's way past six so the bad guys should be long gone."

"We should call Detective Hawk first." I took my phone from my pocket.

"Hold on," Preston said. "She'll just tell you to stay here."

"He's right." Austin curled and uncurled his fingers.

"Fine." I tucked Makayla's laptop under my arm and followed them out of the bedroom. I had to figure out what the broken file was.

We raced downstairs and out to Austin's Jeep. Preston took shotgun, and my mind swirled as I slipped into the back seat.

"I'm really creeped out because somebody had to have hand delivered this letter after I went to get supper." I buckled my seatbelt.

"What time did you leave?" Preston asked as Austin practically skidded out of the driveway on two wheels.

I grabbed Makayla's laptop before it slid off the seat. "Around five-fifteen or so. I had to wait quite a while at the restaurant." I opened the computer and found a timestamp on the picture— 5:33. "The kidnappers were cutting it close if she had to have the file there by 6:00."

"No kidding," Preston muttered.

"Whoever left the message knew Makayla was here alone, that she had the file, and would have time to respond—which means they've been watching us." Where had this person parked? I peered out the window. Down the road, Earl Smith's house had been sitting empty for a while—and his driveway would've been the perfect place for keeping an eye on my house. Goosebumps rose on my arm.

"Mak took the selfie with the note and sent it to her computer hoping we'd find it if something went wrong and she didn't come back." Austin slammed his fist against the steering wheel. "What would someone want with a broken file? That's so stupid!"

I tugged my braid. "Unless broken is the actual name of the file." I perused her computer files, focusing on the most recent ones. There was nothing even close to the name *broken*. "I'm not seeing anything here."

Preston faced me. "Try a search."

I did, and over one hundred files appeared. I turned the screen so Preston could see. "That's helpful."

"Great," he muttered.

I opened the most recent document that contained the word *broken* and discovered a poetry analysis essay, but the word was only mentioned once.

Austin pulled up to the cemetery, and Makayla's Prius and a Camaro were parked next to the wrought iron gate. I set the laptop aside, and we hopped out.

Both vehicles were empty, and no one was milling around the cemetery. I shivered when I remembered Bobbi Sue's statement about the place being haunted, and even though I was mostly certain it was a bunch of baloney, I kept one eye out for a phantom dog.

"Do you know where Floyd Fillmore's grave is?" Preston asked.

"It's the big one with the angel." I pointed to the middle of the cemetery at the monument towering over the surrounding headstones. We entered the gate, passed the weeping willow, and surveyed the graveyard as we walked toward Floyd's headstone.

"Makayla!" the twins yelled in unison.

"She's not here."

I whipped around at the sound of the unfamiliar voice.

Jonas appeared from behind the massive weeping willow.

# CHAPTER NINETEEN

"Where's Makayla?" I glared at Jonas. Preston and Austin took menacing steps toward him.

"I have no idea." His eyes widened as he lingered next to the tree. "She left a message asking me to meet her a little before six. She said it was really important. When I got here, she was gone, and the place was deserted. But she left a note in her car."

The twins and I raced back to Makayla's Prius while Jonas trailed behind. The car was locked, so we peered through the driver's side window. Her phone rested in a cupholder, and a note, handwritten on a small pad, had been placed on the seat facing the window.

Georgia, Preston, and Austin,
I know you guys will be worried about me, but I'm safe. There was something I had to do, and it'll be over soon. Tell Dad and Jill not to worry. I love you all.
Makayla

My heart thudded as I took a step back from the car. "That's almost exactly what Quincy said. How could Makayla do this?"

"Maybe someone forced her to write the note." Fear shone in Preston's eyes.

"That seems more likely." My stomach churned as I swept my gaze over the cemetery. "And why do people keep meeting here, of all places?"

Preston looked around. "It's private and in the middle of nowhere."

"And no security cameras," Austin added.

"It's a brilliant choice," Jonas said. "Even if it *is* creepy."

I drilled Jonas with my glare. "For someone with coimetrophobia, you seem pretty comfortable wandering around." I folded my arms.

"I'm not afraid." He hung his head. "I made it up because I didn't want people to think I'd snuck out to meet Quincy."

Austin glared at Jonas. "Who are you, by the way?"

"Jonas Dawes. I go to Brenneman with Quincy and Makayla." His shifty eyes glanced back and forth at the twins.

"Did Makayla tell you why she was coming here?" I asked.

"No."

Austin and Preston eyed Jonas as if they didn't believe him. *Yeah, me either.*

"Here." Jonas reached into his back pocket. "I'll play the message." He did, and Makayla said exactly what Jonas had told us.

My heart squeezed when I heard the tremor in her voice, but I had to stay focused. I showed Jonas the picture of the ransom. "What do you know about the broken file?"

Jonas scrunched up his face. "Is the file out of commission, or is that the actual name?"

"We're not sure," I said. "But for now, let's assume it's the name of the file."

"This is the first I've heard of it. I'm sorry." Distress lingered in his expression.

What was going on? "Let's check Floyd Fillmore's grave." We hurried to the middle of the cemetery where we inspected the angel monument for the file, but there was nothing there.

"Can you think of any reason why Makayla would have access to a file that had something to do with Quincy?" Preston asked.

That was a great question.

Jonas blew out a breath. "No. Unless they were both involved in something shady that finally caught up with them."

As if they'd choreographed the move, Austin and Preston clenched their fists and stepped toward Jonas. I didn't want to think the worst of Makayla, but had she gotten in over her head? Had she insisted on leaving the tour early because she'd known Quincy was in danger? What if she'd been lying all along?

"Easy guys." Jonas edged closer to the monument. "I didn't mean to insult your sister."

I held up a restraining hand, and they edged back. I had another question for Jonas and wasn't ready to scare him off. "Why do you have a burner phone?"

He flinched and then shoved his hands in his pockets. "I'm not a criminal. Back when I was in high school, I met this girl at church camp. When camp was over, I gave her my number. Big mistake. That chick became a total stalker—texting me all the time. Calling every night. I blocked her number, but she used new ones to harass me. Finally, I had to dump my number and get a new one. From that point on, my dad told me I had to use a burner for strange girls. So, that's what I've done ever since. I meant to give Quincy my real number, but I missed the window before it got too weird to tell her, you know?"

"Totally, dude," Austin said.

"It's brilliant." Preston held out his fist for Jonas to pound. "I'm *so* getting a burner."

With a sigh, I took out my phone and called Detective Hawk.

---

As soon as Preston, Austin, and I had spoken with Detective Hawk at the cemetery and surrendered Makayla's laptop, we returned to my house. The boys had decided that since I was the eldest sibling, the task of informing Dan and Mom of Makayla's disappearance should fall to me. I couldn't really argue. The call was not pleasant.

They vowed to take the next available flight out of Guatemala.

I went to my dining room and stood in front of the chalkboard. After I erased what I had written about Tune Nutritional Supplements, I wrote *the broken file*. I printed pictures of Makayla's and Quincy's notes and tacked them up along with a picture of the ransom demand.

Preston entered and flopped down at the table. "Do you think Mak has a secret life we don't know about?" He rested his head against his fist.

I hadn't wanted to believe Yvonne when she'd implied that Makayla could somehow be involved, but maybe Yvonne wasn't just cynical, and her instincts had been spot on. Makayla had withheld the truth on more than one occasion during this investigation.

"You know her better than I do. Does she have a history of hiding things?" I dropped the chalk in the basket, brushed my hands against my jeans, and joined him at the table.

"Yes." Austin hovered in the opening between my dining room and foyer. "Remember when she was dating that guy her freshman year of college, and she didn't want any of us to know?" He sat next to his brother.

"Right," Preston said. "She never told us who he was, and they eventually broke up."

"I don't think they went out that long." Austin looked back and forth between us.

"Anything else?" I asked.

"She didn't tell Dad when she changed her major from pre-law to professional writing because she was afraid he'd have a stroke," Austin said.

I raised my eyebrows. That didn't seem likely for mild-mannered Dan—even if he was overprotective. "*Was* he upset?"

"No way. He was cool. Our mom was a journalist, so I don't know why Mak thought Dad would be shocked. He never pressured any of us into being lawyers," Preston said.

Austin chuckled. "Good thing, because I don't have the patience for that much school."

"Same here." Preston raised a hand.

"It *would* be cool to be a trial lawyer, though." Austin slapped his palm against the table. "Objection!"

Just when they were showing signs of maturity. But I couldn't be too hard on them since they obviously used humor to cope. "Guys, let's stay focused."

"Makayla's always had a complex about not measuring up in Dad's eyes," Preston said. "It's like she doesn't realize he's hard on us because he loves us and wants us to be the best we can be—at whatever we do."

"But what about the lip ring she got a while back? Dan definitely didn't approve," I said.

"She went through a rebellious phase." Austin unbuttoned his dress shirt.

"Whoa. Easy there!" I looked away.

"Relax. I'm showing off my rebellious phase." He yanked his

shirt open and pointed to the dragon tattoo on his pec. "Dad hates it, but it's awesome, right?"

"Nice." I turned to Preston. "Do you have any ink?"

"Not where I can show you."

"Eww."

"You should see the look on your face." He snickered and pointed. "I'm kidding. I hate needles."

We all smiled but sobered quickly and studied the chalkboard in silence. I despised feeling so helpless. But what was there for us to do? I pressed my fingertips to my forehead.

*Please help us, God.*

About twenty minutes later, my doorbell rang, and when Gus and I answered, Cal stood on my porch. He wore a fitted gray T-shirt and jeans, and my heart skittered.

What had I been thinking, letting him go? "Hey." The doorknob became my lifeline.

"Vanessa told me what happened tonight. Are you going to let me in?"

"Right." I stepped aside and realized the twins were hovering behind me. "I thought you were taking time off."

"That doesn't mean I can't check on my neighbor." He closed the door behind him and eyed Preston and Austin.

*Neighbor.* As kind as his gesture was, knowing I was just the person next door knifed my heart, and I dragged my focus to what was most important—finding my stepsister.

"Thanks. We're fine, and we've been trying to figure out how Makayla's involved in all of this. You might as well have a look at my chalkboard." I pointed to my dining room, and we gathered around the table. "We still don't know what the broken file is or why someone wants it."

Cal ran his hand over his mouth and chin as he took a moment to study my scribbles. "Based on how similar the girls' notes sound, I think they're involved in the same thing."

"Our sister wouldn't do anything illegal," Preston said.

Cal raised his eyebrows. "I never said she would. For all we know, she wrote that note under duress. If you don't want my help, I can go." He motioned toward the door. "I'm taking time off work, so I'm not even here officially."

"We want your help." I shot my stepbrothers a dirty look.

"Have you talked to the other girl who was here the night Quincy took off?" Cal asked.

"No." Why hadn't I thought of her sooner? "Sammi's cousin is married to Quincy's sister, so she might know something."

"Do you have her number?"

"No." I sighed.

"I do." Austin took his phone from his pocket and scrolled.

Of course he did.

"They met when she came home with Makayla one weekend," Preston said.

Funny how he thought he needed to defend his brother. Cal and I grinned at each other. Oh, how I missed that dimple.

"Let Georgia make the call," Cal said.

"No prob." Austin read the number to me.

Preston elbowed him. "Dude, did you ever follow up with Sammi?"

"No, but I totally should've. She's cute."

I stepped toward my living room as the phone rang. I anticipated having to leave a message since she wouldn't recognize my number.

"Hello. This is Buffy Sanders. How can I make your night . . . *special?*" a breathy voice said. Giggles erupted in the background.

Apparently, Sammi and her friends were bored. "Sammi, this

is Georgia Winston. Do you mind if I ask a few questions about Makayla?"

"Ohmygoodness. I'm *sooo* sorry. My friends and I have this thing about messing with unknown callers. We're in the airport waiting for our flight to Florida."

She and Austin *would* get along well. I returned to the dining room. "I get it." I explained who was with me and got her permission to video chat before filling her in on the events leading to Makayla's disappearance.

"Do you have any idea what the kidnappers could've meant by the broken file or why Makayla would've had it?" Cal asked.

"No. I wish I did, but that doesn't sound familiar. Give me a second, and I'll ask around."

The screen went dark, and she had a muffled conversation before returning to our view. "Nobody knows. I'm sorry."

My stepbrothers' shoulders slumped, and Cal turned toward the chalkboard.

Given that my stepsister hadn't always been forthcoming, I had another question I needed to ask Sammi. "Makayla mentioned she and Quincy weren't getting along lately, but she made it sound like it had something to do with Quincy coming in late all the time. Can you think of anything else that might've caused problems between them?"

"They really didn't have much to do with each other." She chewed her lip for a moment and then sat up straighter. "You know . . . a while back—like last semester—Makayla said something about writing a song with Quincy."

"Really. Why?"

"I think it had something to do with entering a songwriting competition. I don't know how far they got, or if they gave up on the idea. Makayla didn't mention it again or give me any more details." She paused as a boarding call sounded in the background. "That's our flight. I *think* I've told you everything I know, but I'll text or call if I remember something else."

"Thanks for your help, Sammi. Have fun in Florida." I disconnected and stared at the guys.

"I didn't know Mak was into song writing," Preston said.

Austin shook his head. "Same here. She doesn't even play an instrument."

I remembered seeing the award certificate for the poetry contest in Makayla's room and considered what Dr. Jackson had said about Quincy's talent. "She wouldn't need to if she was just writing the lyrics and Quincy was composing the music.

"Mak's definitely into poetry." Preston shifted back and forth as if he were winding up, ready to spring.

"What if the broken file is a song?" Cal and I said in unison.

Austin clapped. "I love how your minds are totally in sync."

Preston elbowed his brother.

"I mean, that theory makes sense," Austin mumbled.

I avoided Cal's gaze. "Why wouldn't Makayla have mentioned the song—or working with Quincy?" I didn't want to believe she'd been dishonest with me—again.

"Maybe they never finished or entered the contest, so it never occurred to her," Cal said. "Especially if it happed a while ago."

I could tell he was having the same doubts about Makayla, but I appreciated his attempt to reassure me. "I should talk to Quincy's parents first thing in the morning. I want to see if they know about the song."

"Even though they accused you of trafficking?" Cal asked.

"I'm hoping they'll have calmed down enough to be reasonable."

Cal set his jaw. "You shouldn't go alone. I'm flying out of Indy tomorrow afternoon to visit a buddy, so how about I meet you at the Ashbrooks?"

"Sure. I'd appreciate that."

176

"I'll let Vanessa know everything we found out from Sammi."
He walked toward my front door, and I followed.

"Thanks for coming to check on me—us—because I appreciate it, and we're all worried about Makayla."

"You're welcome."

I gripped the doorknob. "Who are you visiting?"

"Mason."

For a split second, he looked as if he wanted to say more. Or was it my imagination? Did I dare tell him I knew? Yvonne hadn't given me instructions to keep quiet. "Why didn't you tell me about his wife's murder?" I met his eyes.

"Who told—?" He swiped his jacket from the bench. "Never mind. It was Mom."

"Yes." I searched his face for anger but only found sadness.

He ran his fingers through his hair. "You had a lot on your mind with Aunt Beverly dying and your grandpa's wedding and your dad's case. I didn't want to add to your burdens."

"But . . . I would've understood. I could've listened and been there for you." That was what people in a relationship were supposed to do. "I wanted to be supportive."

He put both hands on my arms. "I know. I'm really sorry." Regret flickered in his blue eyes. "I'll see you tomorrow." He dropped his hands and slipped out the door.

Sorrow kept me frozen in place as he walked away.

# CHAPTER TWENTY

"I apologize for how my husband and I treated you the last time we spoke." The next morning, Janet Ashbrook set a tray with glasses, a pitcher of lemonade, and a plate of sugar cookies on the coffee table on her expansive sunporch. It overlooked a pool, outdoor kitchen, and fire pit. "It was truly abominable to accuse you of trafficking. Please forgive us." She smiled at me before letting her gaze linger on Cal.

Had Stuart followed through on the background check and realized his accusations were ludicrous? Would Janet be asking for forgiveness if her husband were here? Whatever the reason, I needed to put everything behind me and focus on Makayla. "I understand you were stressed."

"We still are," she said.

Janet had made an attempt to disguise the bags underscoring her eyes, and her skirt, rose-print cardigan, and pearl necklace advertised her effort at maintaining a sense of normalcy. Her formal attire and living space made me glad that I'd made the extra effort and put on my black blazer and the chunky turquoise necklace that Cal had always liked.

"Georgia can relate to your situation because Makayla disappeared yesterday under circumstances similar to your daughter's," Cal said. "Even the note had similar wording. She told everyone not to worry, but as you know, that doesn't quite cut it."

Janet nodded. "Detective Hawk updated us last night. Do you have any new ideas about what's going on?"

"Possibly," I said. "Do you mind if I ask more questions? Cal is here as my friend since he's taking time off work."

"Not at all. As I told Detective Hawk last night, my husband and I want to find the girls as much as you do." She fiddled with her cardigan's hem.

"Did Quincy ever mention a song called 'Broken'—or a song with that theme?" I asked.

"No." Janet didn't meet my gaze.

"Did she ever talk about writing a song with Makayla for a contest?"

"No. This is the first I've heard of it." Uncertainty filled her voice. "Though Quincy *has* entered her own songs in contests."

"Did she win?"

"No. But I told her not to be discouraged. She's very talented." Janet examined her French manicure, and seconds ticked by.

"Is there something else you want to tell us, Mrs. Ashbrook?" Cal asked.

She smoothed her skirt. "Since we spoke with you last, my husband has informed me that our daughter was far more involved with Elias Kurtz than I realized." She stared out the window toward the fire pit.

My guess had been correct. Stuart had hidden Quincy and Elias's relationship from his wife. "Sometimes children make choices that go against the values their parents try to instill."

"Yes." Janet's chin trembled. "Yes, they do."

Since we were on the subject of Elias Kurtz, there was another angle I wanted to pursue. Tune Nutritional Supplements probably didn't have anything to do with this case, but something was still bothering me, especially now that we were in the Ashbrook's million-dollar home. "Why did Quincy decide to sell Tune?"

Janet ran her hand over the sofa. "After Quincy ran away in high school, my husband cut off her allowance. We paid her college tuition and any other necessities, but Stuart wanted her to understand the value of a dollar. She sold Tune because the flexibility permitted her to work around her class schedule. She also believes the products are beneficial to people's health. Unfortunately, business has dropped off lately, and I suspect the market is tapped out."

It was probably too much to hope that Janet would admit to running Quincy's Tune business.

"Could you tell us about the band Quincy ran away with in high school?" Cal asked.

Janet grimaced. "She was enamored with the drummer in a rock band. His name is Tanner Smith, and he's in medical school now."

"What was the band—?"

The back door slammed. "Janet?"

Stuart rounded the corner into the kitchen and scowled when he caught sight of us in the sunroom. "What're you two doing here?"

Janet shot up and hurried over to her husband. "They had a few questions." She rested a hand on his arm. "It's fine. They're just worried about Quincy and Makayla."

He shook off her hand. "You know how I feel about this. We told that other detective everything we knew last night."

Janet blanched. "Stuart—"

"I want them out of my house. Now." He pointed toward the door.

Cal and I stood.

"Thank you for your time," Cal said.

"And hospitality." I swiped two cookies and followed Cal out the door.

# CHAPTER TWENTY-ONE

I parked next to Cal's Jeep in the William's Home Supply lot and hopped out of my truck. Neither one of us had wanted to linger in Stuart and Janet's driveway, so he'd told me to follow him to the store to debrief.

As he walked around his Jeep to meet me, he was whistling "C is for Cookie" from *Sesame Street*.

I burst out laughing. I probably should've been embarrassed, but my sweet tooth wasn't a secret to my ex-boyfriend.

"How were the cookies?" He pushed his sunglasses up on his head, and his eyes gleamed.

I withdrew a napkin-wrapped cookie from my purse and held it out. "I saved you one."

He chuckled. "I'm good, thanks."

"Suit yourself." I returned it to my bag. "Janet's a good baker. Her cookies rival Taryn's." The comment spewed out before I could stop myself. Breaking news—Nice Georgia was still on the lam.

His amused look made a comeback—along with his dimple. "I

need to price some kitchen cabinets, so let's walk and talk." He motioned toward the store.

"Sure." I slammed my truck door. Walking and talking was perfect. Plenty of built in distractions in case awkwardness decided to pay a visit, and since that trait and I were old friends, that was pretty much a given. "You decided to renovate?"

"I hired Hamlet to update my kitchen and the bathrooms."

I nearly tripped on the curb. *Hamlet?* Why hadn't he said anything? Would they talk about me? *Seriously, Georgia? Life Lesson #829: Not everything is about you.* "I'm sure he'll do a good job." The doors slid aside, and we entered the store.

"Yeah. I checked out the work he's doing on his flip, and he knows his stuff." Cal glanced at me. "He's a nice guy too."

Why was Cal stating the obvious? I'd known Hamlet for years, so of course I knew he was nice. Was Cal making a casual comment, or was he hinting that he approved of me dating Hamlet—if he hadn't changed his mind?

"He'd be good for you."

I commanded my feet to keep moving past the appliances. *Right. Left. Right. Left.* For once, I didn't have to wonder what Cal was thinking. "Really?" I sounded as squeaky as my shoes against the concrete floors.

"Yes. It's obvious he cares about you, and you have a lot in common."

I reminded myself to take a breath. And another. "Tell me about the renovation." That was a safe subject.

"We're opening the kitchen into the living room," Cal said. "It'll give the house a more modern feel."

"Uh-huh. That'll be nice if you have kids someday."

"Don't know if that's ever gonna happen." He strode toward the displays of kitchen cabinets.

"Things not going well with Taryn?" I tried to sound casual, but there was no getting around it. I was flat out nosy—and needed to know if she was the reason Cal was encouraging me to date Hamlet.

"Nope." His jaw twitched.

*So much for the Taryn theory.* "I'm sorry."

"I'm not." He stopped in front of white Shaker cabinets. "I like these."

"They're pretty." And exactly what I would've chosen. I even had them on my Pinterest board of kitchen renovation ideas.

He snapped a picture. My nose started to burn, announcing imminent tears, so I had to think about something else before I shut myself away in the floor-model pantry and bawled.

I needed to focus on finding Makayla instead of my own drama. "Did you think it was weird that Stuart and Janet were on completely different pages about our visit?"

"Yes. I also wonder why Janet tried to hide her husband's feelings." He examined the cabinet's price tag and made a note in his phone.

"Unless she didn't know."

"Or she's in denial."

Janet seemed to possess a special talent for that where her loved ones were concerned. "It's interesting that Janet told us the Tune market is tapped out when Makayla said Quincy had a wad of cash before the tour."

"I'd agree if the Ashbrooks weren't wealthy, but Janet's perspective about the amount of money Quincy made is probably very different than yours and mine." He shoved his phone into his pocket.

"True." I thought of the diamonds she'd worn when she and Stuart had visited my house and the pearls she'd had on today. Not to mention her clothes might as well have come with a neon sign that flashed *expensive.* "I wish we hadn't been interrupted. I really wanted to know more about Tanner Smith." I'd definitely look into him later.

"I agree. Before I leave, I'll call Vanessa to make sure she's followed up with him—and the band." He turned toward the exit, and we strolled to the front of the store.

"Thanks. Are you headed to Cleveland?"

"Atlanta. Mason's been staying there with his grandma ever since they realized Natalie's death wasn't random." He shoved his phone into his pocket. "His parents died when he was seven, and his grandma raised him."

"I assume he's worried about his grandma's safety."

"Yes. And his two-year-old son, Henry's."

I stopped near the checkout lanes. "I'm so sorry. I didn't know Mason and Natalie had a son."

"Yeah."

The anguish in Cal's blue eyes broke my heart. It was so unfair that a precious little boy would grow up without his mother. "You can count on me to pray for justice."

He brushed a strand of hair back from my face and looked me straight in the eyes. "I appreciate that."

For a few seconds I held his gaze and forgot everything that'd gone wrong.

Then, he glanced at his watch. "I need to get to the airport." We stepped through the sliding door into the sunshine and walked toward our vehicles in silence.

"Thanks for your help today." With shaky fingers, I dug in my purse for my keys when we lingered behind my truck.

"That's what friends are for. Take care." He got in his Jeep and waved.

*Friends.* My heart squeezed as I watched him drive away.

---

I made it home from Indianapolis without driving off the road. Tears had blurred my vision more than once, but the closer I'd gotten to my farm, the more I realized I had the answer I'd been praying for. Cal and I were friends, and I should be thankful for that development and that he'd clearly given me reason to stop hoping we'd reconcile.

It was time to quit dwelling on the past.

With my mind on Makayla and Gus at my side, I entered my office, did a quick online search for Tanner Smith, and laughed aloud at the large number of results. What had I been thinking? I added the words *drummer* and *band* to the name.

Though it showed fewer results, I didn't find anything helpful.

I leaned my elbows against the desk and buried my face in my hands. What now? Would Sammi know the band name? If she didn't, maybe she could ask her cousin. I found her number and sent a text.

> Do you know the name of the band Quincy ran away with in high school? If you don't, will you please find out? Thank you!

I drummed my fingers against the desk and waited for a few agonizing minutes, but when she didn't respond right away, I leaped up.

The day had turned warm, and since playing in the dirt always eased my frustrations, I rushed to my room, donned a pair of overalls, and went outside to till the soil in my backyard garden bed. I'd be able to plant carrots, peas, and onions before long.

The wind painted faint ripples across the pond, and the grass was slowly shedding its dull brown in favor of a tentative green. I tethered Gus nearby so he could get some fresh air and watch me work. He ran back and forth barking at the ducks before settling in the grass with a chew toy.

I strolled to the backyard shed next to my garden bed. I took my phone out of my pocket, tapped my favorite playlist of choral music, and put in my earbuds. While the beautiful melodies and harmonies soothed me, I spun the padlock on my shed and rolled out my rototiller.

As I worked the soil in my garden bed, I pondered my unanswered questions about Quincy and Makayla. I walked the length of my garden and turned. Even if the girls disappearing had something to do with a song they were writing, how did Elias's death figure in?

Why did Quincy's disappearance, Makayla's disappearance, and Elias's death all take place at cemeteries? That had to be significant. But why? If Jonas were guilty, why would he draw attention to himself by lying about coimetrophobia—and then go on to kill Elias at a cemetery? That made no sense. Clearly, I was missing something important.

My phone buzzed, and I yanked it out of my pocket. Sammi had responded.

**Boneyard Rebels. Creepy, right?**

Definitely. In spite of the afternoon warmth, goosebumps rose on my arms. I fixed my gaze on the northern horizon in the direction of Fillmore Cemetery.

Cemeteries—a.k.a. boneyards.

I shaded my phone from the sun's glare and searched for information about the Boneyard Rebels.

The first hit was Parker Curtis's website. *Weird.* I tapped the result and skimmed his bio.

*Parker's music career began during college with a rock band called Boneyard Rebels. Parker was the lead singer, earning the nickname Boneyard Boss.*

BB. My heart thudded.

*When the band broke up, Parker returned to his first love—*

*country music. He formed the Parker Curtis Band in 2016 and transformed himself from a rock singer to a country star whose original, heartfelt songs resonate with audiences everywhere.*

Quincy knew Parker Curtis from her time following the Boneyard Rebels, which meant she'd met him that night at Fillmore Cemetery. But how did Elias figure in?

Whatever was going on, I had to call Detective Hawk and tell her. I paused the music and scrolled through my contacts.

Gus woofed as a thick arm captured my waist, and a gloved hand covered my mouth.

I writhed in the assailant's grip, and Gus strained against his tether. I bit the leather glove, but my captor drove a fist into my side. Groaning, I flailed my elbows, aiming for my attacker's gut. I lost my grip on my phone, and it thumped into the dirt.

Gus howled.

A pinch bit my bicep, and I gasped as my captor injected a drug. *No, please, God.* I twisted and kicked but my movements grew sluggish until I couldn't command my limbs to move.

Within seconds, my yard dissolved to black.

# CHAPTER TWENTY-TWO

I needed to open my eyes but couldn't. It was too hard. Relaxing was easier. Something was wrong. No, I was floating on a raft. A summer day at Grandma and Grandpa Smith's lake cottage. Gentle waves. Warm sun. But didn't I need to fight? Why? Sleeping was . . .

So.

Much.

Nicer.

---

My grainy eyes fluttered open, and nausea assailed me. I pressed my hand against my mouth, flopped over on my side, and squeezed my eyes shut.

Something bad had happened. But what?

I fought against a fog-filled mind. I'd been working ground in my garden. Gus had barked. And then . . .?

The attack.

I forced myself to lift my head and observe my surroundings.

Four cement block walls in a space that couldn't have been more than eight feet by eight feet. A metal door. I sprawled on a simple camping cot, but someone had provided a travel pillow and a light blanket that wasn't thick enough to keep away the chill permeating this claustrophobia-inducing space. In the opposite corner was a ten-gallon bucket with a toilet seat.

*Ick.*

I dropped my head back on the pillow. My stomach roiled, and bile rose in my throat. I should try to make it to the makeshift toilet.

But it was so far away.

I slid onto the damp concrete, crawled to the bucket, willing the nausea to pass. I took a deep breath . . . and another. No. Wishful thinking.

I emptied my stomach into the bucket.

Propping my back against the cement wall, I tried to shake off my confusion. Quincy disappeared. Elias was murdered. Makayla had taken off. Parker Curtis—BB—was somehow involved.

Now I was here. But why? How had someone figured out I was close to the truth? And where in the world was here?

I stared at the block wall as time ticked by and my nausea diminished. With each passing moment, my grogginess subsided, but increasing panic replaced it.

I examined my body. Other than being drugged, I didn't appear to have been hurt. Was someone watching? Goosebumps riddled my arms, and I searched for nooks and crannies where someone could've hidden a camera, but I didn't see anything.

I patted my overall pockets. My kidnapper had taken my phone—which wasn't surprising. No—I'd dropped it in the dirt.

I stood on shaky legs and pressed my ear to the door. Straining, I detected faint footsteps but couldn't be sure where they were coming from. I turned the knob—just in case but it held.

*Life Lesson #10,958: Always carry a lock-picking kit.*

I shuffled to the cot and plopped down. If I'd been faster, I could've placed my call to Detective Hawk. I hoped Preston and Austin would think it weird that I was gone when I'd said I'd be home working. Not to mention I never tethered Gus outside unless I was working nearby.

How long had I been here? It had to have been between two and three o'clock when the kidnapper had snuck up on me.

I reassessed the door. Even though it was solid metal, the lock wasn't any more secure than the simple one on my bedroom door. I patted my pockets to see if I'd stashed anything in them while I was working that would be useful, but I hadn't.

I upended the cot and ran my hand over the metal frame, searching for any loose pieces, but the cot was new. A rough edge snagged the skin on my thumb, drawing blood, and I swiped my finger on my overalls.

*My overalls.*

I unfastened the bib and examined the strap. If I could get a metal piece off the strap, I might be able to bend it and turn the lock. I tried tugging the piece off, but the material was too thick. Kneeling next to the cot, I rubbed the material against the rough edge. It took a lot of swipes, because I still felt like I was moving under water, but the durable material began to fray. I pulled on the hole to help it along and resumed sawing. Continuing this pattern, I finally got the material to rip, and I held a metal piece in my hand.

It would take some doing to manipulate the metal, and the task seemed overwhelming. Closing my eyes, I longed to succumb to sleep. Not now. I had to get out before someone came back for me. When I bent the piece straight, I finally had something I could try to maneuver the lock with.

I inserted the metal piece into the lock and twisted, but it held fast.

*Please help me, God.*

I tried a few more times before a faint click sounded. "Thank you, Lord." I slid the metal piece into my pocket and peeked out the door at a narrow hallway leading to a set of stairs at the end. I beat it out of the room as fast as I could, even though I still felt like I was moving through a vat of glue. A large window next to the stairs displayed a small recording studio.

What *was* this place?

I trudged up the stairs, and when I reached the top, I caught my breath and pressed my ear against the door. The *Jeopardy* song filtered through, which meant I'd been locked up for hours, because that show came on at seven-thirty.

At least, it came on at seven-thirty at home. With all the time that'd passed, I shouldn't assume I was still in central Indiana. Holding my breath, I turned the door handle. *Creeeaaak.* I cringed and squeezed my eyes shut.

*No, no, no!*

I froze. Seconds ticked by. When no one came, I edged into an empty industrial kitchen. I closed the door and tiptoed across the black and white tile floor. The exit was on the opposite wall, and a window in the back door displayed fading daylight. I shivered.

Great. If I made it out, I'd be running through a strange place in the dark.

I passed between an eight-burner gas range and a stainless-steel prep counter with giant pots and pans stacked on the shelf underneath. A large serving window was open to a dining space with rows of tables. On the far end of the dining hall was an elevated stage with a screen hanging in the middle. American and Indiana flags stood on either side.

At least I hadn't been dragged out of state. I slumped against the counter. Was this a camp? I looked into the dining hall again, hoping to see something on the wall that would give me a clue.

Goosebumps rose on my arms. Hadn't Stuart Ashbrook said his wife volunteered at a music camp? Camp Win-something. Had they abducted me because of the questions Cal and I had asked? Were he and Janet capable of kidnapping if it meant protecting Quincy?

I searched for a phone hanging on the wall but didn't see one.

"Avoiding a lawsuit is ideal, so I still support the deal," a muffled male voice said, causing me to jump. "She's almost got it ready."

Lawsuit? And who was *she*? I considered cracking the door to see if I could identify the man, but it wasn't worth the risk. I knew one thing—the man wasn't Stuart Ashbrook. The voice was deeper than Stuart's, but I couldn't be sure it wasn't Parker Curtis.

"We lucked out when that Kurtz guy turned up dead."

Who would've benefitted from Elias's death?

"Take care," he said.

Refusing to waste another second, I slipped out the back door and into the woods, my feet squishing and slithering in the mud. I stumbled forward in a slow jog until I doubled over with a stich in my side. Taking a deep breath and vowing to get an actual membership at Fitness Universe if I survived, I tried to get my bearings. The setting sun clued me in to directions, but unless I could figure out *where* I was, that wouldn't be helpful.

On heavy legs, I stepped over fallen trees and moved toward a cluster of cabins in the distance. If there was a trail leading away from them, I could find my way to a main road for help. I staggered to the three log buildings that were arranged around a firepit and benches.

I didn't stop but followed the tree-lined path that led away from them. Now that the sun had vanished, the creepiness factor in the woods had multiplied by about twenty as darkness invaded. I whipped my head back and forth, while praying my captor wouldn't realize I was missing. I hadn't exactly been careful blazing my trail over the soft ground.

Ahead, I spotted four cement-block buildings with green metal roofs, and I ducked behind a sycamore tree and did a little reconnaissance. The buildings were dark, but between two of them, I identified a road in the distance. Judging from the noise, there was plenty of traffic. Surely, I could get someone's attention.

But first I'd have to pass through a large clearing with zero trees.

I pressed my hand against the sycamore tree's bark and reconsidered my plan to flag down a passing car. A better strategy would be to find a phone and call for help. One of those structures had to be an office, and there would surely be a landline.

This seemed like a better choice because there was no guarantee a driver would stop to help, and if someone did, it'd probably be the only serial killer within a thousand-mile radius.

Because there was no luck quite like Georgia Rae Winston Luck.

That should be Life Lesson #10.

I sucked in a deep breath, darted out from behind the tree, and stumbled across the clearing with "Silent Running" playing on a loop in my head. I chose the largest of the four buildings, but the back door was locked. I wasn't going to take the time to pick it when there was a glass pane.

Next to the cement stoop, I found a medium-sized rock. I struck the upper corner of the window until the glass shattered at my feet. Reaching in, I flipped the lock.

Mildew and stale coffee lingered in the hallway, and I passed through the first door. Hanging on the paneled wall above a dented metal desk was a *Camp Winland* sign. A phone nestled among stacks of papers, and my shoulders slumped in relief. I lunged for the receiver, but there was no dial tone.

With shaking fingers, I followed the cord to see if it was plugged into the wall jack, and it was. I removed and reinserted the cord before trying the phone again. Silence. My heart plummeted.

Fantastic.

"Hello?" a muffled voice yelled. "Is somebody there?"

"Makayla?" I dropped the phone into the cradle.

"In here!"

I followed her shouts into the hall and located a locked door. I reached for the metal piece from my overalls, turned the lock, and burst into the windowless room.

Makayla sat at a small desk facing a laptop. Her hands were bound behind her back, and her legs were tied to a metal chair.

"Georgia!" Her terrified, blue-green eyes met mine. An angry welt marred her cheekbone, and her pink Rainbow Brite T-shirt displayed a bloodstain.

"Are you all right?" I knelt beside her.

"Yes. Sorta. Not really." Her voice trembled. "How'd you get here?"

"I was kidnapped and just escaped the dining hall basement." I examined the ropes with multiple knots binding her hands and ankles. "Who did this?"

She looked up at me, her eyes welling with tears but blazing with fury. "Quincy."

# CHAPTER TWENTY-THREE

Tears spilled onto Makayla's cheeks. "I went to Fillmore Cemetery because I thought I was helping Quincy. Someone—I think it was a man—grabbed me from behind, and the next thing I remember, I woke up here, and she's forcing me to finish this song we started writing together."

"'Broken'?"

"Uh-huh. It's about a loved one dying." She took a shuddering breath. "She told me yesterday if I didn't write faster, she'd provide extra motivation . . . and . . . I'm trying . . . but I always write my poetry and lyrics in a journal, and I'm not used to using dictation . . . and I'm so sorry because I'm sure that's why they nabbed you." She ended with a sob.

"Try to stay calm. I'll get you out." I fiddled with the ropes around her wrists. Someone had done thorough work on the binding. "Has Quincy or the guy she's working with checked on you lately?"

"Quincy was here like an hour ago." She sniffed. "I haven't seen anyone but her this whole time."

Quincy's partner would surely realize I was missing before

too much longer, and she could pop in at any minute. "I don't suppose that laptop is connected to the internet."

She shook her head.

I wedged my nail into the first knot and tried to loosen it, but it wouldn't budge. "I'll be right back." I rushed to the office, hunted down a lone pair of rusty scissors, and returned to Makayla. My mind whirred as I worked at severing the rope with dull blades. "Why is 'Broken' so important?"

"I asked, but she didn't answer." She tugged the ropes.

"Hold still. When I was in the dining hall, I overheard a man on the phone talking about avoiding a lawsuit. Is Quincy in legal trouble?"

"I don't know!" She sounded like she was about ten seconds away from full-on hysterics.

"Okay, okay. After you were kidnapped, I learned Parker Curtis's nickname is BB—Boneyard Boss from his time as the lead singer of the Boneyard Rebels. That's the band Quincy ran away with in high school." I freed her hands. "What if Quincy made a songwriting deal with Parker, and she's about to get sued because she can't deliver?"

Makayla rubbed her irritated wrists, and being partially free appeared to ease her panic. "Maybe. She's terrible at writing lyrics. That's why we partnered up in the first place. We were going to enter a contest, but we got busy and didn't finish. But Parker Curtis? Why would he need *her?*"

"Good question, but there has to be something big, or she wouldn't have abducted you." I sawed the ropes binding her right leg and considered the man's words about Elias. *We lucked out when that Kurtz guy turned up dead.* "How would Quincy have benefitted from Elias Kurtz's death?"

She swiped teary cheeks with the back of her hand. "Kimberlee Samson told us Quincy and Dr. Kurtz had a falling out over money because she owed him for Tune products, but other than that, I don't know."

"We assumed their disagreement had to do with Tune, but maybe it didn't." I tore the ropes away from her right leg.

"Hold on." Makayla put her hand on my arm. "Dr. Kurtz wrote music."

I recalled the line in his online biography that mentioned he was a composer. "Did Quincy ever collaborate with Elias?"

"I don't know. When Quincy and I were writing 'Broken,' she mentioned working with somebody before, but she changed the subject when I asked who." She stretched her freed leg. "If it was Dr. Kurtz, that would explain her evasion. Besides, the song he performed at the Brenneman talent show was good—like it could've been a major hit."

*A major hit.*

I cut the ropes surrounding her left leg and reconsidered Kimberlee's words. *"She owed him and refused to pay him back. It really hurt him."* Had Kimberlee misunderstood the conversation? She'd only heard Elias's side.

The music from "Refund" played in my head. *Repay each day I dared to care.* Parker Curtis had been in the music business a long time, and after years of struggling, he'd recently had his first major hit. "What if—and this is crazy—Quincy and Elias co-wrote 'Refund'?"

Makayla drew a sharp breath. "Parker claims he wrote that song about his ex-girlfriend."

"What if he didn't?"

"Why not give them credit and tell everyone he could relate to the song? Singers use songwriters all the time."

I plucked away pieces of frayed rope. "What if Quincy and Elias offered the song for no credit because they were trying to get started in the business?"

"I guess they could've made a ghostwriting deal. Parker

would pay them up front for the song—but they wouldn't get credit or royalties. Quincy and Dr. Kurtz both would've had to agree to it."

"What if they didn't, and Quincy sold the song to Parker without Elias knowing?" I unbound her left leg.

She stood and swayed. "Dizzy." Gripping the chair back, she closed her eyes briefly and continued. "If Dr. Kurtz could prove he helped write the song, that'd be grounds for a lawsuit."

I pocketed the scissors and turned toward the door. "And if I were Parker, I'd sue Quincy for deceiving me." I considered the note Makayla had found in Quincy's dress. *You can't ignore this deadline.* "What if Quincy promised Parker another song in exchange for not suing her, and she was going to use 'Broken'? It wasn't like she could turn to Elias for help." I peeked out at the hallway, and it was clear.

"Parker agreed, but when she couldn't finish, I was her last resort."

I motioned for her to follow, and we crept down the paneled hall.

"Right," I whispered. "Quincy may've found a solution for herself, but Elias was still a threat to Parker."

"So Parker killed him . . . and Quincy might've helped."

Except something major didn't fit. "Parker had a concert in Chicago on Saturday night." I calculated times. "Elias was murdered between one and three in the morning. The show probably ended around eleven. With the time change, he'd lose an hour coming to Indiana. Unless he flew in a private plane, he would've barely made it to Richardville in time." I stopped at the backdoor and peered out at the darkness engulfing the camp.

"I read in a magazine that Parker hates flying." She opened the door, and when it creaked, we cringed. "Quincy must've acted alone."

"I doubt it. She's had help this entire time." I thought of the man I'd overheard on the phone.

"If it's not Parker, it has to be someone who really cares about him—and his career."

"And who could've passed her the note at the chorale concert." Only one person fit that description.

"Lukas Dawes," we whispered in unison.

"Brava," a male voice said.

We whipped around.

Lukas blocked the hallway—and pointed a gun at us.

# CHAPTER TWENTY-FOUR

"Please let us go. Makayla will finish the lyrics and send them to Quincy." I jumped in front of her.

A burst of cynical laughter spewed from Lukas's throat. "You know too much."

Makayla inched inside the office door.

"Get back where I can see you, or I shoot!" Lukas shouted.

She edged closer to me.

"Why would you do this?" I was having trouble comprehending how Brandi ever had feelings for this guy. She hadn't been kidding when she said he'd changed.

"I took Parker from a struggling rock musician to a country star, and I couldn't let Elias destroy everything."

"Why didn't you pay Elias for the song and to keep his mouth shut instead of murdering him?" Makayla looped her arm around mine.

"When we found out Quincy had sold the song without Elias's knowledge, we did," he said. "But it wasn't enough. Elias knew the song was a hit, so he came back for more. If we refused, he was going to sue Parker. I wasn't going to let that happen, so I let him think I was meeting to make another payment and . . ."

He looked so proud of himself, I half expected him to blow on the gun barrel. "Does Parker know?" I asked.

"He probably suspects, but when I told him we got lucky that someone offed Kurtz, he agreed. Quincy had a meltdown when she found out I'd killed him, though."

When I'd met Lukas, he'd seemed like a loving, invested brother. "You didn't come to the chorale concert because you care about Jonas. You needed to contact Quincy."

He swiped his beard and adjusted his grip on the gun. "I adore my little brother, but I had to deal with a problem. Quincy wasn't answering the burner phone I'd given her, and her deadline had passed. When we met at the cemetery, Parker agreed to give her another week to finish a new song, or he was going ahead with the lawsuit. He has a soft spot for Q." He grimaced. "She and I came here, and I stayed to make sure she finished."

"And when she couldn't, you helped her lure me out," Makayla said.

A door slammed.

Quincy breezed in, holding a plastic bag containing two syringes. "I've got the drugs." She stopped next to Lukas.

"Good," he said. "These two have figured everything out."

"What's in the bag?" My pulse hammered.

Quincy met my gaze. "Fentanyl. You're about to overdose in the infirmary." She gazed down at the dirty carpet.

My gut lurched.

"How'd you get your hands on *that?*" Makayla's eyes were wide.

Quincy shuffled her feet. "Stop with the questions."

"It's not like we can call the police to burst in here and save us," Makayla mumbled.

Quincy shoved the drugs in her purse and removed a gun. "I

met a dealer when I was selling Tune, and he slipped me a password for what he thought was a secret product line of illegal drugs. It's not true, but I kept his name in case I ever needed something." She closed the gap between us and pressed the gun into Makayla's side, jerking her away from me.

"We heard the Forza 12 products are an urban legend." I cringed when Lukas dug his fingers into my arm and hauled me toward the back door.

"Good work, Detective Winston." Quincy followed, steering Makayla forward.

"Why'd you cut Elias out in the first place?" I stopped myself from adding that she could've saved herself a ton of trouble.

"Elias never would've agreed to ghostwriting. He wanted the glory—and royalties. I tapped out my Tune market and needed quick cash to pay off my credit cards. Parker'd been trying to make it big for years, and 'Refund' was perfect for him."

"Elias wasn't going to sue you?"

"He was . . . too in love with me to do that." Her voice cracked.

"Quincy, you don't really want to do this, do you?" I asked.

"I refuse to go to prison."

"You'll get caught and spend more time locked up than if you'd turn yourself in now," I said. "Besides, Makayla and I don't do drugs. How are you going to explain our overdoses?"

"I can totally convince people Makayla has a secret habit, since I lived with her."

Makayla glared at Quincy.

"That might work for Makayla, but no one will believe I had anything to do with drugs," I said.

"Then we'll just dispose of your body elsewhere." Lukas opened the door, letting in a whoosh of cold air. He prodded me outside, and my feet crunched over the broken glass on the back stoop.

Quincy and Makayla followed us toward another cement block building as Lukas pressed his gun into my side to remind me not to try anything. My fingers brushed against the scissors in my pocket that were no match for a gun.

*Lord, what do I do?*

Along with darkness, a tomblike silence had fallen over the camp. Lukas forced me onto the infirmary's crumbling cement porch.

*Sing praise.*

I didn't question it and chose the first song that came to mind. "In the morning, when I rise," I sang.

"Shut up!" Lukas hissed. But he froze next to the door.

I ignored him, and Makayla joined in with her strong alto, our voices blending in perfect harmony. "In the morning when I rise."

"Be quiet!" Quincy yelled, but she didn't move.

We sang louder. "In the morning when I rise. Give me Jesus."

"Make them stop!" Quincy shrieked.

"Give me Jesus."

"Do it yourself." Lukas clawed my arm. "You've got a gun."

Still holding Makayla, Quincy shoved her gun in her purse. "This is *your* fault. I loved Elias, and you killed him." She removed the drugs but fumbled with the plastic bag, trying to open it with one hand. "Elias didn't deserve that."

"Give me Jesus. You may have all this world. Give me Jesus."

"Sometimes you have to make sacrifices," he said.

"Sacrifices? We're talking about someone I loved!" Her face twisted with rage.

"Oh, when I come to die," I sang, and Makayla joined with tears flooding her eyes. "Oh, when I come to die."

A syringe slipped through Quincy's trembling fingers and clattered against the cement. She swore. "Help me!"

Lukas stepped forward, dragging me with him. I met Makayla's eyes.

We fell silent.

When Quincy bent to grab the syringe, Makayla swiped the purse from Quincy's shoulder. I turned and drove my knee into Lukas's crotch. He let go, doubled over, and toppled sideways on the uneven concrete.

I lunged forward and wrenched the gun from his hand.

With her hands raised, Quincy screamed and sank against the building. "Please don't shoot." The she buried her head against her knees and sobbed. "I'm sorry. I'm so, so sorry!"

Lukas curled into a ball and groaned as I held the weapon on him. "Makayla, call 9-1-1."

# CHAPTER TWENTY-FIVE

After the deputies from the Webster County Sheriff's Department led Quincy and Lukas away from the camp, Makayla and I gave our statements to Detective Ryan McCloud in the main office building's front room. His kind eyes and patient demeanor put us both—especially Makayla—at ease as we described what'd happened.

He also contacted Detective Hawk when we told him about Elias's murder in Richard County and assured us that Quincy and Lukas would be brought to justice. Detective Hawk had already been looking for me, because Preston had reported me missing after finding my phone—and rescuing a frantic Gus.

Now we were sitting on an old wooden church pew waiting for Preston and Austin to pick us up. Mom and Dan were speeding home from the Indianapolis airport.

"I still can't believe Quincy was going to kill us." Makayla rubbed her wrists where the ropes had left a raw band and fixed her gaze on a bulletin board—empty except for a multi-colored star border. "What made you think to sing?"

"I prayed about what to do, and God brought that to mind—in part because you told me to pay attention in church on Sunday."

"Seriously?"

"Yep." I ran my hand over the pew's smooth wood. "I've been having a hard time with the Cal breakup, and God reminded to praise him in my difficulties."

"I'm glad he did." Her voice quivered.

"Me too." I gave her a squeeze. "You're an awesome sidekick, by the way."

"Thanks." She managed a weak smile.

"Presty, we've been usurped."

"What's up with that, Austy?"

The twins hovered in the doorway and opened their arms—and they'd probably string me up me if I ever made it public knowledge—but they definitely had tears in their eyes. We rushed over for hugs.

"Nobody's been usurped," I said. "We're all one big team."

---

The next morning, I awoke to a peaceful house. Gus had refused to sleep in his crate and was still snoozing at the foot of my bed. The night before, Mom and Dan had taken Makayla home to Richardville. Austin and Preston had offered to stay with me, but since the danger was over, I passed. I'd detected a bit of dismay when I declined their protection.

Once I got moving, I decided I needed a fix from Latte Conspiracies—for two reasons. First, because of my recent onslaught of guests, I was out of coffee, which almost never happened, though I was frequently without decent food. Second, Bobbi Sue was sure to tell everyone she knew about the events involving Makayla and me, and I wanted to ensure she'd broadcast accurate information.

Okay. There was a third reason by the name of Hamlet Roswell Miller, and I wasn't even sure he was working. But I hoped so.

When I arrived in town, I found an empty space across the street from the coffee shop, and I parallel parked. The sunny morning was a reminder that planting season was approaching quickly, and the very thought put a ripple of excitement in my stomach.

A bell jingled, and Detective Hawk strode out of Latte Conspiracies with a large coffee cup in hand.

She waved when she saw me. "Georgia, I'm glad I ran into you because I've been wanting to talk to you. How're you doing after everything that happened yesterday?"

We stopped in front of the shop. "I'm all right. Makayla was pretty shaken up, though."

"It'll take her some time to get over being betrayed by her friend."

"Yes, it will. Do you have more questions about the case?"

"No, no." She brushed a strand of auburn hair out of her face. "This is personal."

"Okay." Did this have something to do with Cal? We stepped aside as a few people passed.

"I owe you an apology."

"Why?"

"I unloaded on you about Cal without hearing your side. I know you cared about him and wouldn't have ended things without a good reason."

"I'd expect you to take his side since you work together."

"I know, but that wasn't fair, and the protective part of me got riled up when I saw how upset he was after the two of you split."

"I wish he'd have told me about what happened to Mason's wife, so I could've been there for him, but he shut me out."

She nodded. "That would frustrate me too. Anyway, I talked to him about what happened to you yesterday, and he was more than a little relieved that you're okay. I'm sure he'll check on you soon. He really values your friendship."

*Friendship.* One more confirmation that I needed to forget the past and move ahead. "Have a nice day, Detective Hawk." I turned toward the door.

"Georgia?"

"Yeah?"

"Please call me Vanessa again."

———

After I got an Area 51 Latte and gave Bobbi Sue the scoop about my adventure, I chose a table near the window. While I sipped coffee, I read online articles about Lukas's and Quincy's arrests. This case was receiving national attention because of the ties to Parker Curtis. He'd already lawyered up and refused to talk to the media, so time would tell if he'd truly known what Lukas had done on his behalf.

"What am I going to do with you?" Hamlet slid into the chair across from mine.

"Put me in a bubble." I set my phone aside.

"I don't think so." He reached for my hand and squeezed it. "I'm glad you're okay."

"Thanks. I'm ready to give my detective skills a break for a while. I just want to focus on getting my crops planted." I smiled —and hoped it could be classified as demure. "And saying some magic words."

His face lit up. "Are you sure?"

"Yes." I felt peace about taking this next step.

"Wonderful!" He grasped my hands. "Georgia Rae Winston, I realize it's short notice, but may I take you to dinner tomorrow night?"

I feigned a sigh. "It *is* short notice. I'm not sure I can work you into my incredibly busy social calendar."

"I see." His eyes glimmered. "Perhaps next Saturday would be better."

The edge of my mouth twitched. "I'm kidding. Tomorrow would be perfect."

"Excellent. I'll pick you up at seven." He stood and kissed my cheek. "Have a lovely day." He strutted back behind the counter —and I couldn't stop grinning and thanking God for the gifts of life, health, and friendship.

I really was one lucky woman.

---

Don't miss Georgia's next adventure in *Deadly Hideaway*. Stay in touch by subscribing to my e-mail newsletter at www. marissashrock.com and get the latest on my new releases.

As a thank you for subscribing, you'll gain access to *Deadly Homestead: A Georgia Rae Winston Mini-Mystery and Other Short Stories*.

If you enjoyed *Deadly Harmony*, I'd be very grateful if you'd leave a short review to help me spread the word about my novels.

# ABOUT THE AUTHOR

Jenni Mansell Photography

Marissa Shrock is a survivor of many awkward blind dates and many years of teaching middle school. Both provide excellent inspiration for her fictional yarns.

Since childhood, she's loved to read a variety of genres, so her own work includes dystopian thrillers and cozy mysteries. She's the author of the Emancipation Warriors Series and the Georgia Rae Winston Mystery Series. Her debut novel, *The First Principle*, was a Carol Award Finalist.

Marissa enjoys playing golf, building elaborate LEGO creations, and traveling to new places. Her home is in Indiana, where she's surrounded by corn and soybean fields. Visit her at www.marissashrock.com.

ALSO BY MARISSA SHROCK

The Emancipation Warriors Series

*The First Principle*

*The Liberation*

*The Pursuit*

*The Agitator: A Novella*

Georgia Rae Winston Mystery Series

*Deadly Harvest*

*Deadly Holiday*

*Deadly Heritage*

*Deadly Harmony*

*Deadly Hideaway*

*Deadly Heartbreak*

# CREDITS

Editing by A Little Red Ink

Cover Art by Seedlings Design Studio

Marketing Copy by JR2 Marketing & Advertising

Cimelia Press Logo by Race Point

Beta Readers: Mary Shrock, Brad Shrock, and Katie Briggs